CW01263090

No part of this publication may be reproduced, stored in a retrieval system, or transmitted in any form or by any means, electronic, mechanical, photocopying, recording, scanning, or otherwise, without the prior written permission of the publisher, except in the case of brief quotations within critical reviews and otherwise as permitted by copyright law.

NOTE: This is a work of fiction. Names, characters, places, and incidents are a product of the author's imagination. Any resemblance to real life is purely coincidental. All characters in this story are 18 or older.

Copyright © 2020, Willow Winters Publishing. All rights reserved.

Seth & Laura

W Winters

USA TODAY BESTSELLING AUTHOR

*This book is dedicated to everyone who feels
as if they're at their worst.
It's okay.
There's always a way out.
Tomorrow may not be better,
but better is coming.*

I promise you, you won't be down for long.

From USA Today bestselling author W Winters comes an emotionally-gripping, romantic suspense.

I fell for someone I shouldn't have.

I'm not the only person to ever do such a thing. I know that. And I'm not an awful person for desiring his touch, his kiss, his everything... but I knew I shouldn't have indulged.

There's something about knowing it's wrong that tempts me that much more. The seduction became a game with higher stakes than any before him. In fact, it was only ever him.

The thing is, I knew I shouldn't. Now that the game is over and the pieces have fallen...
I know I should have just walked away.

There's no way out of the wreckage.
That doesn't change the fact, that I wanted him more than anything. I still want him more than anything.

Tempted To Kiss

Prologue

Seth
Eight Years Ago

With every day that passes by, I hate myself more and more. Only when she's not around, though. When she closes the door and the crisp lonely air reminds me what a prick I am, that's when the resentment creeps in. I have that sound memorized now. The sound of her closing the front door of her house is unmistakable. It's not like other doors. It's heavier, I think, and it has to be older because of the ragged groan it gives. Then there's a pause and a click, followed by the shuffle of the metal chain brushing against the door as she locks it at the top. It's so high up, she has to get on her tiptoes.

Then there's nothing but silence and a hollowness in my chest that reminds me why she's on the other side of it while

I'm out here in the cold, waiting for the dark to set in.

The only saving grace I have is that when the light of daybreak peeks over the city's skyline hours later, I know she's waking up with every intention of letting me back in, giving me the only chance I have to make my sins right.

She should hate me for what I've done. She should loathe my existence.

Instead she unknowingly takes my hand and offers me the only peace I have in this life. If she knew the truth though... none of this would exist. These moments with her would only ever be a dream. Then I'd wake in the dawn, hating myself a little less than I hate myself now.

There are two sides to my life: The first is the side that protects Laura and holds on to the threads of her trust. Power, greed, and killing comprise the other.

That's what drives me back to her every morning. I like to pretend I can keep the dark side of myself at bay, if only for her.

The look in Laura's eyes right now as I stand in her kitchen, waiting for her to tell me I should go—I've seen it a million times before. The carefully restrained lust echoes in my own gaze. I'm certain she sees it. Just as I see it from her. I know what keeps me from turning my fantasies into reality. I don't know what keeps her from acting on our mutual desire. Maybe she senses what I'm hiding. Maybe there's a deep-seated instinct that warns her away from me.

If only it were that easy to avoid the bad things in life. Simply sense them, these situations, and turn them away. How wonderful this world would be if it were so easy.

"Thank you, Seth," she says and her soft voice is gentle and sweet. There's a hint of shyness that stays with her when she lets me in. Her skin flushes a little brighter, although this time of year, it can be blamed on the wind from outside. We're in her home though, and her cheeks are a touch rosier than they were before we came in here. I have no right to let her innocence stir the flames of desire inside of me.

The microwave beeps, alerting Laura that her hot chocolate is done. "You sure you don't want one?" she offers over her shoulder. She's looking more at me than she is at the hot mug in her hand, as if she's asking me something else entirely. She quickly sets it down when I shake my head and leaves it there, running her hands down her thighs and biting just slightly into her bottom lip.

Leaning against the doorframe to her grandmother's kitchen, I note that no one's home. No one else is here to make sure she's all right. Her grandmother works herself to death and her father…

"Do you want to…" her voice trails off and a warm blush creeps up to her high cheekbones. Nearly up to her hairline. Her nervous laugh brings an infectious smile to her tempting lips. They're the color of sweet, perfectly ripe berries. Maybe whatever berry her lips were made from were truly the forbidden fruit that condemned mankind to hell.

"Do I want to... what?" I question teasingly, crossing my arms and taking her in. It's taken a long damn time for her to warm up to me. It took months for her to ask me to come inside. It's been a few more months now and every day is easier, lighter. Until she's gone and then I remember.

Laura picks at the hem of her large, cream-colored sweater. Her leggings make her look so relaxed and at ease. It's been forever since I've seen her like this. No more red-rimmed eyes, no more tearstained cheeks. Almost a year, and she's seemingly whole.

She closes the distance easily enough; her strides don't give anything away. I'm only aware of how quick she is to get to me from the rapid thuds made by the pads of her feet. Shock and surprise consume me as her dainty hand grips my forearm, her nails barely touching my skin, teasing me. *Thump*, my heart pauses. She rises up on her tiptoes, barefoot and all, and presses those sweet lips to mine. *Thump*, my heart races with need and hunger.

At first it's soft and gentle, a peck on the lips and nothing more. Maybe someone else would take it as a thank you, as testing a boundary, or flirtatious innocence. It's anything but that to me. The barest of affections from her elicit a storm of want and need that floods my blood with desire. Even the feel of her breath so close is like heaven, so close I can almost taste it. Adrenaline races through me and I deepen the kiss.

My arms uncross and wrap around her small waist before I know what's happening.

The kiss is searing, branding my soul as she moans into my mouth. When she parts her lips, I take it as an invitation, giving in to the perverse thoughts I've had for as long as I've known her. The air turns hotter around us, everything blurring and turning into nothingness. That's all life's ever been for me, nothing without her.

I make a vow to myself as she parts from the kiss, her eyes half lidded, her fingernails digging into my skin to ensure I keep my grip on her. She breathes heavily as I promise myself, she'll never know.

I'll kill the man who tells her what I've done. I'll kill him for taking her away from me.

Chapter 1

Laura

I wish I didn't know. I wish Seth had never told me. I wish I'd never pressed him.

Once you tell someone a secret like the one he told me last night, you can't take it back. More than anything in the entire world, I want to go back to that moment and beg him not to tell me. That little secret changed everything.

My cheek rests heavily on my fist, my elbow propped up on the metal table. It's cold and I can't stop rocking my right leg, which is crossed over the left. My muscles are tight and sore from sitting like this for so long, but I can't get comfortable either way.

All I can think about is how I wish I hadn't pushed him. I wish he'd had the sense not to tell me.

All the wishes in the world don't mean shit as I bite away at my thumbnail in this far too cold empty room. Does that make me weak, or less of a woman? To wish I simply didn't know something so awful and life altering? If it does, so be it. I just want to go back. I don't want to know any of it.

The air conditioner keeps coming on and each time it does my heart leaps. It's accompanied with a loud click, that fills the quiet space. It scares the shit out of me every time it clicks on. I haven't slept in God knows how long now. I know that's not helping, but how could I possibly sleep in this room? It's not designed for comfort. I haven't taken my medicine either and the beating organ in my chest runs wild. It doesn't want to be in this interrogation room any more than I do.

My thumbnail is jagged and rough from biting it down to the nub as goosebumps spread across my flesh and my foot nervously taps against one of the metal legs of the table.

Four chairs, a table and a long-ass mirror at eye level on the wall to my left are all that are in this room. I'm no fool and I'm fully aware it's a one-way mirror and they're watching me.

Officer Cody Walsh is watching me.

Maybe he's waiting for me to break. The question is: how long will he wait?

The door opens suddenly, ripping me from the trance I'd been in as I stared at my own reflection. From the scrubs I put on yesterday morning, to my red-rimmed eyes, blotchy from smeared mascara, I look like hell. Or rather like I've been to hell and come back to tell the tale.

Again my heart reacts at a sudden unfamiliar noise as the door opens, thumping and loudly protesting this man's existence.

Cody Walsh will always look handsome, I'm sure of it. There's a charming air that surrounds him as he lets the door close behind him, a coffee in each of his hands. He's not dressed in his uniform, clad only in faded jeans and a crisp white collared shirt. Classically handsome fits him well. Wholesome, even. With neatly trimmed hair and never more than a five o'clock shadow on his face to pair with his gorgeous blue eyes and pearl-white smile, he's a good-looking man to say the least. A little older, but good-looking nonetheless.

"You didn't sleep," he comments with compassion in his tone. I wish he weren't compassionate. That's how he gets me and I'm so aware, yet so in need.

I fall for it. My dreary night lends itself to a need for sympathy. The ball of emotions clouds my vision and I let my hand fall over my eyes, scrubbing them and reminding myself that I can't say anything to anyone, no matter how long I'm meant to wait in this room. Anything I can think to say to Walsh in greeting jumbles itself at the back of my throat. I suppose some piece of me would rather choke on the words than give them to the man who arrested me.

"The guilty ones sleep." Walsh's voice remains casual, friendly even. It's unavoidable to look him in the eyes as he walks over to me, confidently and nonthreatening in the least. "You didn't and I knew you wouldn't," he says as he places a cup of coffee beside me. It smells like cinnamon and he must notice how I gaze down at the cup longingly the moment it hits the hard, unforgiving table. Which is the only thing that's been my company for hours. I shift in my spot and suddenly realize how sore my elbow is from resting in the same position for so long.

The white paper cup is innocuous, the black lid standard, but it looks and smells like heaven to me.

Wrapping both of my hands around it, the warmth is everything. "Do you intentionally keep the room cold?" I ask as my shoulders shake with another click of the air conditioner turning back on. I knew it was coming, but still wasn't ready for the sudden sound. It's less of a shock with Cody distracting me though.

Officer Walsh looks up at the vent only a foot from me before turning, leaving the room without a word and then coming right back. The constant breeze is no longer present and he gives me a weak smile although his eyes don't reach my own. "My apologies."

The concrete floor protests in a loud screech as he pulls out the metal chair across from me. I take a sip of the coffee, unable to refrain any longer. The least I can do for myself is consume some sort of energy. I haven't eaten in a long damn time since I didn't take my lunch break on my last shift. I don't know if the coffee is decaf or not, but the warmth alone is welcome. My eyes close and the lack of cool air against them grants me a small sense of peace. It's short-lived, but it was there for a moment.

Walsh gestures to the coffee and says, "Cinnamon crumb cake or something like that. It was the special of the day. I don't know how you take it."

"It's perfect," I find myself saying as I open my eyes and stare straight ahead at the blank wall. I add after the tick of the clock, "Thank you."

He nods in acknowledgment but then what he's holding steals his gaze from me. There's a folder in his grasp and he puts it on the table but doesn't open it. Splaying his hands, he places them on either side of the folder and looks down at it as he speaks, rather than at me.

I wonder what it contains. Maybe evidence they found. Statements they took. Maybe it's all blank papers and the man across from me simply wants to make me scared. At this point and from everything I've learned in my lifetime, any of those options are possible.

"There are three ways I see this playing out." With the first bit spoken and my heart pumping harder, Walsh looks me in the eyes. He clears his throat and says the first option: "You're tried and convicted for the murder of a cop."

I swallow, the remaining cinnamon-flavored coffee suddenly making my throat tight. My pulse seems weaker and my head feels lighter at the thought. I could spend the rest of my life in prison. How is that justice? My conscience plays flashes of my life for me, each moment I got away with something wrong, something I shouldn't have done. Justice and karma are quite different, aren't they? When I push the warm cup away and fold my arms over myself, the cop continues, his voice a bit stronger. "The second option: I let you walk away and you go back to the man who had you take the fall."

I bite the inside of my cheek to keep from speaking up to defend Seth and I know Cody Walsh sees it. The metallic taste of blood is awful, but uttering a word right now would be worse. I have to work hard to school my expression to neutral. I won't say a word. I haven't got a damn thing to say to him. If I so much as mention Seth, they could bring him in. He's shot, he's not okay.

Seth would have never meant for me take the fall. Never. I all but pushed him out that window. He may not be a good man, but he's a good man to me. My heart sputters as the vision of Seth confessing to me last night comes back. I hide it, burying it beneath the image of him taking a bullet for me. How am I supposed to think straight when my world is so tilted?

My eyes close with the silent prayer that Seth's all right. That he did what I told him to. My eyes open again while wondering: what are the odds that he already knows I'm in here? They have to be high. He must know. If he's able, he'll save me. I know he will.

"Or the third option," Walsh continues. "Charges are pressed against you, you go to jail, and Seth, with the help of the Cross brothers, pull their strings to get you out."

Hope flutters at the thought of the last scenario being the case. That will happen. That is the most likely outcome, right?

I've never known Seth to abandon me. He can be crude, an asshole. He's lied to me and done so many wrong things. Worse than just wrong. He does things that are horrible, things that some say would send him straight to hell. But never once has he abandoned me. He'll go through hell, commit all those sins ten times over, just to save me. It's one of the things I'll always love about him. He's a damaged man beyond repair, but he wouldn't let me suffer if he could stop it.

The rustling of Cody's jeans as he readjusts in his seat brings my gaze back to his. "None of those instances lead to justice." Justice sounds funny. Like it doesn't belong in that sentence, let alone this conversation. "I think the third is the most likely, if you're wondering."

I have to blink away my surprise at his admission.

"Given the experiences I've had so far in this city, the men you hang around have a way of protecting themselves and I," he pauses to suck in a breath, his brow rising before falling back into place. He lets out the breath and continues, "I hadn't realized how close you were to them until recently."

Tick, tick, my heart beats faster than the clock. I want

to tell him that I'm not close to the Cross brothers, but I don't say a word. Remembering that not speaking is my best defense. If they charge me, I'll get a lawyer. Right now I'm in holding and having a lawyer won't change that. I'm aware of my rights.

"I don't know what will happen to you after you leave here, and that worries me."

The concern he displays nearly makes me respond that I'll be safe with Seth, but that's none of his business. Not only that, but I don't know how I could ever be with Seth again. My throat tightens at remembering what started this domino effect.

I have to clear my throat before I can tell Officer Walsh I don't have anything to say other than the initial statement I gave. It was self-defense and I hardly remember anything at all. I told them everything happened so fast and I was so scared that I think I blacked out. It was the best excuse I could come up with at the time and now I'm sticking to it.

"The thing is, one of the men was a cop. So even if they get you out of here, the investigation won't stop."

Out of a nervous habit, I grab the coffee and sip. I'd rather drink than speak.

"There are men who aren't in the back pocket of the Cross brothers. Men who also break the law and they'll go around it to see someone pay for Officer Darby's death."

"Are you threatening me?" I ask and the shock is

unrestrained, new fear coming to life.

"No. Not at all." His response is quickly spoken, his eyes wide like he wasn't anticipating my reaction in the least. The next thing he says is spoken with strength and sincerity. "I'll do everything I can to protect you." My question obviously shook him and his answer was quick and sincere. "I don't want you to be involved. It can't end well for you if you are."

My nod is imperceptible as I absently scratch my nail against the paper coffee cup.

Words sit on the tip of my tongue. An explanation that the cop is obviously in the wrong, but now I question everything. Seth shot first. The masked man had the gun raised though. I've played it so many times in the back of my mind that the sequence of events is a blur and for a split second I'm not sure if I am remembering correctly. Inwardly I shake my head. Seth shot first. I know that truth. But those men threatened me with deadly force, the cop included. If I could go back, I wouldn't want Seth to wait and see whether or not the trigger was pulled. If he had, I might be dead.

It has to mean something that I was threatened in my own home. That has to be important. The most important thing. All the words tangle at the back of my throat and I can't swallow.

They strangle me.

Cody Walsh looks down at me with such sympathy, I nearly crack and ask him to tell me if it matters. It has to matter, doesn't it?

My ass feels numb as I readjust in my seat, suddenly aware of how uncomfortable I am. My eyes are dry and burning. Of all the fatigues and pains, they hurt almost the most. Almost.

My fingers spread across my chest as I feel the faint pumping of my battered heart. Nothing could hurt worse than this.

I haven't forgotten what Seth confessed. The pain is proof of that.

"Let me help you," the good officer suggests as if he can. Nothing can help me. I won't betray Seth. I barely survived the first time. I wouldn't be able to look at myself in the mirror if I do it again. With weary eyes, I close them lightly, refusing to answer.

I have to sniff, breaking the silence and suddenly feeling stuffy. I haven't cried and I'm proud of that. In the face of everything crumbling around me, I don't feel the need. What's done is done and now I wait. It's all I can do.

"The death sentence is a possibility in this state, Laura. You don't want to risk this," he stresses.

"I don't have anything to say, Officer Walsh," I say and my voice is eerily calm. At my decision, the click of the air conditioner returns. I keep my eyes on Cody, but he moves his to the vent.

Although it genuinely tugs at my lips, I let out a small humorless laugh when he turns to look at the door, as if he'll see through it to whomever has turned the air back on.

It's a long moment before he says, "We can hold you for forty-eight hours without charging you."

I don't look at him. The metal table holds all my attention because it plays my life back for me like a movie. From the first time I laid eyes on Seth King to the sight he was last night. Forty-eight hours in here. I can make it that long. The *tick, tick, tick* of the ever-present clock calms any anxiousness I have. It's a balm to my torn soul, even if my hands do shake in my lap.

"Laura." The way the officer says my name grips my gaze, forcing me to look him in the eyes. They're the most tranquil of blues and riddled with concern. It would be touching if I didn't feel so much peace at the thought of simply being alone. "He killed one of us. They aren't going to let this go."

I don't respond. I don't have anything to say and I've already made that clear.

"Please, let me help you," he beseeches.

My hands are hot when I press them to my eyes, breathing in deep and feeling the weight of everything pulling me under what feels like the roughest of tides.

I've been beyond help for quite some time. Forty-eight more hours isn't going to change that.

CHAPTER 2

SETH

I never thought I'd be grateful for the cold. I've always hated how cold it gets on the East Coast; it numbs the pain, though. Most of it. So the cold is something I need, something I focus on to keep me moving.

At least four men are guiding me, shoving me forward and keeping my arms pinned behind me. Listening to everything, every breath, every step they make—that's the only information I have to go on to figure out how many there are, how big they are and what I'm up against.

Without the cold, I'd be burning hot with the need to react. The clang of the metal grates beneath my feet sparks recognition immediately. Thank fuck for that, because I can't see a damn thing with the bag over my head.

The grates on the edge of the parking lot let me know my location without a doubt. I'm away from Laura and her place. That is the only silver lining to this fucking ending. They're moving away from my Laura. At least she'll be all right. The thought is calming in the best and worst of ways.

The sound of crickets, along with leaves blowing indicates the woods behind Laura's apartment complex are to my left. The longer I'm out here, the more information I have, and the more settled I become. The telltale whoosh of a van door opening sounds to my right. I don't react; I don't let them know I'm even halfway with it.

According to the men taking me in, I reek of whiskey, I'm bleeding out and there's no way I'll make it.

Let them think I'm drunk. Let them think I'm slowly losing consciousness.

I want the elements of shock and surprise to be on my side when I get my opening.

This is on Marcus. The men in her place, these men waiting outside making sure it went down like it was supposed to. I know in my gut Marcus set it up. He's a dead man. Every fucking person who's involved is a dead man.

I'll fucking kill him but odds are he's going to kill me first. Unless I get a single opportunity. I just need one.

"Get him back, get him to talk. That's all you need to worry about," a gruff tone says. He doesn't hide his voice and I almost give a start at realizing I recognize it. I recognize the way he coughs and I practically see him doing it. I've seen him close his fist and cover his mouth with it. He doesn't do well with the change of season. He said that once. I know it's him.

"I didn't sign up for this," one man protests, his voice hushed but I hear it.

The response is pushed through gritted teeth. "We have one job, get him there alive so he can talk." I can hear a shove, a scampering back. "Do your fucking job."

The hair stands up on the back of my neck. I followed this prick, I watched him for weeks. He's one of Marcus's men. Tall and gangly, but he's got strength hidden in his thin frame. He was by the bridge, lugging crates. No one would view him as a threat at first if they happened to come across this man. Average in everything with the exception of height. His dark eyes and towering stature are the only marked traits.

"What if he dies on the way?" another man asks lowly in a whisper, as if he's hiding it from my knowledge. Concern is evident and I don't know if there's credence to it or if all this pretending I've been doing, making my body heavy and groaning with the pain is a good enough act to convince them I may very well be dying.

He speaks again in single syllables, loud and distinct with anger clearly evident. "Get. Him. There."

I've been listening ever since a gun was shoved to my temple. I only know the tall man with the gruff voice. We identified him as Steven Davis. Barely on the grid, but identifiable from a previous criminal record.

A hard shove to my right shoulder forces me to stumble and I exaggerate it, falling to my knees on the asphalt. As the man who held my arms grabs my shoulder, I test whether or not the ropes are tight on my wrists. They're not. It's a sloppy job that was done quickly. Only meant to aid whoever it is behind me. They may buy him some time if I were to try to fight my way out, but the knots will loosen.

"Get up," the deepest voice says. It came from the one closest to me. The way he grips me and easily flings me up makes it obvious he's got weight to him. I dub him: the muscle.

"Keep him alive." The words are gritted in a hiss and I immediately feel a prick in my arm as my footing is finally getting settled. It's a shot of something. "That'll help."

The grimace on my face can't be seen, and I'm grateful for that. It's so fucking cold and my head feels light.

Footsteps move farther away even though the hard grip on my arms remains. Three pairs of them. A car door opens and then another.

The four men around me has decreased to maybe two. At most. Two men are within reach. If I had to guess, the others are walking around the vehicle.

If I don't try now, it may be the last time I ever see Laura. Laura.

My body reacts before I can think. Throwing my head back, it slams directly into the big man, The Muscle, who had my arms restrained behind me. He yells a slew of curses and without missing a beat I turn and shove my full weight into him. The ropes burn as I work them, doing my damnedest to wrest them free. It works. The relief is slight, but it's there as the coarse rope falls beneath my hurried feet.

The screams of "Get him!" trail at my back. I don't wait; I run as fast as I can. My muscles scream and I barely get the black bag off my head before I hit the edge of the brick wall that surrounds the dumpsters. My right shoulder slams directly into it, knocking me off-balance and spinning me around. *Fuck!* The pain is fresh and brutal from the hit.

In a quick glimpse I see everything. The single light in Laura's parking lot, the all-white van with no windows, and the four men racing toward me with a look of dread in their eyes. One of them is most definitely Steven Davis. Our eyes lock and I know he knows that one of us will die soon.

"I'll shoot," one yells, stopping to point a gun and I take off. He's a heavier guy who's hard to see this late at night, but his build, his voice, they're etched into my mind. Every single one of them, I'll remember for as long as I live. Or, at least, as long as they live.

Revenge won't happen tonight. This is my only chance to run.

Agonizing pain courses through my limbs, every muscle coiled and screaming with the plea to stop. I sprint through it, past the dumpsters, past the complex and down to the woods. The smell of dirt is fresh, like an autumn rain mixed with crisp auburn leaves.

It's dark, too dark to see much of anything between the thick grouping of old oak trees. The fall leaves crunch beneath my feet as I whip around the dense forest. The bark scrapes my forearm. Fuck! The sting only adds a touch more pain to my already battered body. My breath forms clouds in front of my face, the only warmth I can feel at all.

Run. My heart pounds in my chest. Run as fast as I can.

My pulse hammers and my gut twists inside of me. I can't fail. I can't let them catch me.

Three. Two. One. I hurl myself down the left side of the woods where the drop-off is. I knew it was there. Letting myself fall down the steep hill, tumbling and crashing through sticks and gnarled roots, I prepare for the large overturned tree. It looks like it fell some time ago, but the roots took hold and it made its home in the side of the hill.

The second my body smacks into the trunk, I cling to it, gritting my teeth so I don't scream out from the sudden blunt force to my chest. It knocks the wind out of me but with shaking arms, I move my body around the tree and stay silent, hunched down in the darkness on the dirt floor and listen. My breathing is sporadic and heavy.

Quiet. Stay quiet. Stay still. The trembling aftermath is a constant. Aiming to control it, I close my eyes. I prepare. I listen.

They don't throw themselves down. Instead they run,

stumble and try to keep from falling down the steep hill. I can't tell how many there are. They move past me, even though I swear my heart is hammering so loud they should have heard it.

Two men pass by with precision and haste, following the trail. I catch them out of the corner of my eye and if only they turned to look, they'd see me. The moon is brighter now. They keep moving, making their way as quickly as they can, but it's damn near impossible with how steep the cliff is.

There are two more. I can faintly hear one a moment later, the twigs snapping under his weight. He's quiet. He's got to be the heavier man. The one who aimed the gun. Far quieter than the other two, despite his weight. He goes slowly, tracking and being patient. I don't dare swallow or move an inch until he's far past me.

Even then, I know there's a fourth. There's another man looking for me and I refuse to move until I know where he is.

I take the moment to assess, my eyes fully adjusted to the darkness and look up between the scattering of leaves still clinging to their home, at the small bits of light the canopy provides.

As quietly as I can, I lower my hand to my side, my teeth grinding against one another when I feel the soaked shirt. My breath is stolen from me at the small movement. How did I run? How did I run through this shit?

More importantly, how much blood did I lose?

My head rests against the tree and I blink away the memory of getting shot. I can barely breathe, I can barely stay up straight, exhaustion pulls me down and whispers that I should give in. I should let go. I reach in my pocket, but my phone's gone.

Fuck. Fuck! I can't die like this.

I need to go. I need to tell Jase what happened. They have to save Laura. The cops were there. She needs help and protection. I need to know what's happening.

Crack. Snap.

Branches break behind me. Thin ones and my eyes focus straight ahead as my back stiffens. The rust-colored leaves are eerily beautiful as I overhear the horrid words from one end of a conversation.

"If we don't get him, we can get her."

Steven Davis.

Her. Laura. Each realization is like dominoes falling.

My instinct is to react and with the small movement up, my body revolts. The need to vomit is strong from the sharp gutting pain. I hate myself. I hate being weak. *He's threatening Laura.* He will suffer a slow and painful death. But first, he'll give me three other names. The slight satisfaction is immediately drowned out by fear at hearing more of his one-sided conversation. I strain to hear the voice on the other side of the phone, but it's impossible.

"Yeah, she's in custody," he says. "Make sure they don't

let her out and plant someone in the cell with her." My blood runs cold, freezing every inch of me down to the marrow of my bones.

"Make it clean, she doesn't need to suffer."

No. No, they can't hurt her. She didn't do anything. My body begs me to plead with the man. I've never begged for anything but I can't fight him, I have nothing left.

Thump. My heart pounds and my gaze shifts to the ground.

There's a set of stones on the edge of the hill. A path of them. It's a foot long, maybe longer and the rocks are strategically placed. They follow along the side of the steep hill, as if it leads somewhere. Hopefully, somewhere with a phone.

I have to save Laura. It's the only thing that matters.

The man breathes heavily, gasping for air behind me and I stare at the closest stone, imagining grabbing it and slamming it into the back of the man's head. It'd be heavy enough. Could I do it fast enough, though? If I can't, there will be no one to tell Jase. No one will know she's there, no one will know they're going to kill her. She has to live. I have to save her.

My right side screams in pain and I nearly pass out from my first attempt to stand.

Fuck. Fuck!

I hold my breath, waiting for the prick to get out of earshot before I crawl and climb my way down the path.

I can't die until I know she's okay. Wherever this path

leads will have a phone. I just need to get to Laura before they can. I breathe a silent vow to save her. I'll kill them all before they lay a finger on her.

The promises I make silently to her are the only thing that keeps me going.

Chapter 3

Laura

I keep finding my hand pressed against my shirt as if I can calm down my freaked-out heart. All the while, my body rocks steadily on the metal bench. It's fine.

I'm fine. My arrhythmia has never really been an issue. It's just a butterfly feeling in my chest.

The first time I remember this feeling, the sporadic fluttering in my chest, was when I stood in the doorway of my grandma's house, lying to Seth. I remember it so clearly. I even held my shirt the way I am now.

The memory makes me smile; it's a welcome distraction.

The door creaked open and I stood there in my thin pajamas as the wind shook through the house. I folded my arms over my chest because I wasn't wearing a bra, and although I knew that when I opened the door, I hadn't anticipated the cold. The wind blew by though, forcing the door to open wider and I struggled to keep myself covered while still keeping a handle on the door.

"Why aren't you dressed?" Seth's eyes roamed down my body leisurely. It may have been cold that day, but he made me feel hot from head to toe. Ever since we'd had sex, with one look he turned my knees weak.

I wasn't his girlfriend though and I couldn't keep going like that. He didn't want anything more from me and I was convinced I was only going to get my heart broken. At the thought, my heart did an odd thing. I opened my lips to lie to him, but my heart protested.

I gripped it, telling it to shut up and calm down. That was the first time I remember feeling my heart acting up.

"You all right?" he asked.

"I'm sick," I said and the lie came out tight. I just need to be away from him right now. I need a chance to think. Because when I'm around him, I can't think right.

He stood there in jeans and a leather jacket, a jacket he'd put around my shoulders a week ago. I don't know how I could have lied to him back then so easily, especially with the way he made me feel. "I'm not going to school today."

He nodded, a short nod, and asked if he could do anything for me. Even as I shook my head he kept asking, "No homework to turn in?"

It physically hurt to lie to him, but I didn't want him to keep walking me to and from school. I didn't want him to feel obligated to do anything at all with me. My heart was all sorts of tangled up in his touch and the way he cared for me... it wasn't right. He never made a single move; I did it all. I knew what that meant. That's not how love happens. I could easily see a new woman walking by, catching his eye, and then I'd be gone.

When I shut the door, I hated myself. I spent the next twenty minutes doing what I'd done all morning, figuring out how to get the hell out of Tremont. I didn't have much money and I didn't have any family outside of this town, but I knew Grandma would let me if I found a way.

That's what I was doing when the knock sounded at my door. My jaw dropped when I looked through the peephole.

There Seth stood, with a plastic bag from the corner store a few blocks down. I couldn't unlock and open the door fast enough.

"What are you doing here?" I questioned him as if he was crazy and it only made him smirk.

He lifted the bag and said, "I got you soup and a few other things." I didn't offer for him to come in, but he did anyway, like he belonged there. As if he was supposed to be there in that moment, taking care of me.

The little pitter-patter in my chest lifted, trying to stop any words of protest I had from coming out.

"Sorry you're sick, Babygirl, but I hope you like chicken noodle soup." As I stood there, my back falling against the door, I watched him make his way to my kitchen, fully prepared to take

care of me. I knew in that moment, I was utterly and completely in love. I was certain there was no way I could ever run from him. I knew I should. I knew it with everything in me.

The butterfly feeling hits me again, only this time it's harder and much worse than it was before. I don't remember it ever feeling like this, so painful that I can't ignore it.

It's probably just from the lack of sleep and stress. There's nothing here to distract me either; I'm focusing too much on it. The squeezing sensation and irregular, weak beats are okay. I'm sure it's fine. Why didn't I take my medicine?

Panic attacks are not uncommon and I sure as hell have a reason to dissolve into one. Seth was shot and I don't know if he's dead or alive. That's my first thought. My first reason. As if being charged with the murder of a cop isn't reason enough.

I would give anything for Bethany to be here right now. I could tell her everything and she'd make sure that Seth was all right and he knew. My one phone call went to her voicemail though. It's ludicrous that every situation keeps getting worse and worse.

A whimper leaves me, a pathetic sound as I hunch over, pressing against my chest even harder when the next pain hits.

I tell myself it's fine again and open my eyes to see a stainless steel toilet with no lid across the small cell from me. That's the only other object in this room. A metal bench and a toilet. Simple enough I suppose. At least it's not cold in here. There's a man at the end of the hall, so at least one other person is around and the lights are dim, probably because it's early morning or very late at night. I don't know either way, because there's no clock and the man doesn't speak.

I thought he'd gone for the longest time until I heard that horribly loud beep that goes off before the heavy doors open. He came from nowhere, his boots shuffling across the cement to open the doors, tell someone something lowly, I couldn't hear a thing, and then they shut again. He walked back to his post and silently stayed there.

The dark blues of his uniform complement his brown skin and light blue eyes. He must be mixed race, with one parent white and one black maybe, to have features like that. Cleanly shaved, he's handsome because of the sharpness of his masculine jaw. Any other day, I'd smile at him, make small talk. But the attractive police officer is not my friend. Not in the least.

He's the only company I have. I could tell him about being on the verge of a panic attack but the idea of him ignoring me, or not doing anything at all hurts more, making my heart thump wildly in protest. I'm not a criminal, yet I'm here. In a fucking holding cell.

The jail cells are nicer. I've been back here more than a few times for patients. I've hated that oppressive beep of the locked doors since the first time they made me shudder. I hate the sound even more now.

The jail is not unfamiliar with psychiatric patients.

Oftentimes, a mental illness goes unidentified until a patient has done something worthy of being locked up. Behind bars they can't hide their symptoms and it's so much easier to see and identify.

So I've been here before, accompanying a doctor to diagnose or treat someone. It was never a good feeling. The sound of the doors opening and closing gave me nightmares the first time I came here.

I thought it was because of my family history, my father being a drug dealer and all, that I had such an aversion to jails. That's ridiculous though, no one likes a jail. No one likes the reason a jail needs to exist and they certainly don't want to be inside of one.

Sure as hell not behind these bars. Not alone in this cell, apart from the silent guard who I can't even see because he stands at the far end, tucked away.

The last patient I saw here died in her cell. She wasn't in the holding area; she'd been in jail a while for assault, I think. The cells are past this hall and through two sets of doors. I remember it well. She didn't tell anyone she was seeing things. She didn't tell them about the voices. It took another inmate being scared shitless for the guards to be informed.

The voices in my patient's head told her to hurt herself, which they'd done before. She told me about them in therapy. She went from thinking the pills caused the voices, to knowing she needed the pills to shut them out.

Maybe she was lonely in that cell. Maybe that's why she didn't say anything.

Either way, when I got to her cell, we were all too late. I can still see her wide eyes, staring blankly ahead when the orderly rolled her over. Death has a certain look to it. It stains your memory and waits there, refusing to leave you be.

"I'm on medication," I say, finally giving in to the sudden fear and the nurse in me, calling out to the man I know is here even if he's silent and out of view. I have to shake away the memory of that woman. I don't remember her name and somehow that makes me feel even worse. "I think I need my medication," I call out. My words run ragged as the pain gets worse.

I can't die in here from a heart condition because of my pride or shame. I can't die in here at all. I need to know Seth's all right.

Just breathe. Everything's all right. *He'll be all right.*

The hall is quiet behind the bars and I haven't seen a soul in a few hours, I think. So when the guard doesn't respond right away, I start thinking he's actually left this time. I have no idea how much time has passed. I couldn't sleep, not even with the blanket they left in here. I can't do anything but blink away horrible visions, go over every regret, and notice how erratic my heart is right now.

"Please!" I cry out and I'm immediately met with the sound of a heavy door creaking open and even heavier boots smacking against the cement.

The guard. I finally catch sight of his badge and it says Walters. He's accompanied by another man who looks like he's in his fifties and is a little too round to work in the field. He stops behind the bars, so I can't see his name tag. Walters is quick to speak into a walkie-talkie on his sleeve while the other man stares at me. His wide eyes are the same shade of brown as his khaki pants. "Miss?" he questions. "Did you say medication?"

His brow is pinched and concern is etched there. It's only then that I realize I haven't stopped rocking and my hand is a fist around the fabric at the front of my shirt.

"What's going on?" I recognize Walsh's voice along with the door beeping and opening again. The pain is unforgiving as I catch sight of Walters's back as he speaks to Walsh. Again, the other man just stares at me, maybe bewildered, maybe wondering if I'm acting.

A cold sweat breaks out along my skin and my head feels faint.

"Walsh." His name comes out stronger than I thought I could say it. I force myself to let go of my shirt and stare down the long hall until the officer finally looks at me. The gaze from Walters burns into me. He never takes his eyes off me. Even when he gives a command to the unnamed guard who then departs, Walters's steely blues stay pinned on me.

"Are you going to let me go?" I manage to squeeze out the

question the moment Walsh comes over to me. "I need to get out of here."

The pain in my chest spreads and it feels like it's in my throat, hollowing it out but also burrowing inside of it. I can't describe it. I've never felt this before. My hand drops as I sway forward slightly, closing my eyes and focusing.

"I need to get out of here," I say again, louder and with enough forlorn sincerity to make sure Walsh both heard me and knows something's wrong.

"That isn't going to happen," Walsh says and he sounds resigned to the fact. "The state is pressing charges."

My heart skids to a halt. No longer tumbling uncontrollably, it simply stops and I sit there, shocked and waiting. Waiting for it to start again.

"I wanted to release you." *Thud*, my heart's weak but it's working. "I told them to watch where you go if we released you."

"So nice of you," I whisper because that's all I can manage. It hurts to talk. My chest is so tight. I'm fighting to breathe but trying to look strong.

What did he say?

I can't even focus. Officer Walsh said something. He's fuzzy. The room is so hazy.

"Open it up!" he screams, his grip tight on the bars across from me. "Who did she talk to?" he questions the silent Walters.

"No one, I swear. No one saw her! This doesn't make sense." Whether he's my friend or my foe, Walters's eyes flash with fear. I see it. I'm sure of it. At least he doesn't want me to die. It's a minor consolation as needles dance on my skin.

Their voices blend and blur. I'm upright one moment, then in the next I'm falling. Walsh grabs me, his fingers in a bruising hold. I can't breathe, but I can't move either. I can't swallow.

I'm blinking though. I can blink for a moment.

"You aren't getting out of this, Laura." Walsh uses my first name but it's shaky. My lips twitch in an effort to respond. Nothing comes out though. Still, I can blink. Even as I get colder and fear wraps itself around me. "Not this way," he adds as he shakes his head.

"Medic!" Cody Walsh screams. His skin reddens, panic overriding every other expression. "Medic," he screams out again behind him, laying me down on the hard cement floor.

His hands push against my chest, and then his mouth is on mine. It takes me a long moment to realize it's CPR. I can't breathe. I'm not breathing.

"Is there a pulse?" a new voice says. I barely hear it as my vision turns black.

My hearing is the last sense to go. "I'm losing her!"

Chapter 4

Seth

A thick coat of dirt and blood covers my hands. That's why the knob slips at first. I tell myself that's why it slips and not because I'm on death's doorstep.

The rusted metal turns in my hand on the second try and even that small movement sends a bolt of pain through my right side. Still on my knees, I lean against the doorframe as the backdoor to the worn, wood-paneled lodge creaks open. Someone built a house back here. The three windows in front were the only light in the darkness on this side of the forest. I could barely see it in the woods but as I came closer, I knew there was someone here. The red paint is long worn off and the back porch is barely stable, but at the very least, the lights are on.

It has to be hours since I've been shot. Hours of losing blood. Hours of fighting to stay alive. All I can hear is the rush of my breath as I sneak into the backdoor of the house.

The last thing I need is to get caught, or to unknowingly walk into the enemy's territory. I don't know shit about who lives here or how far I've traveled. It feels like miles and miles.

I swallow thickly, forcing myself to stand up and lean against the wall. I'm quiet enough, but the dirt comes with me, serving as evidence of my arrival.

The creak of the door is muted in the kitchen. The old linoleum floors haven't been swept in a long damn time. It takes three steps for me to close the distance to the counter and reach for a neatly folded dishrag. The kitchen is darker than I was expecting, faintly lit by a single light from the room beside it, most likely the living room since a dining room can be seen to my left.

The blood is still damp on the gunshot wound, but some of the skin has dried to my shirt. I grimace as I pull it back, revealing that the bullet passed through me cleanly.

Sucking in a breath, I press the dish towel to the wound both on my front and back and then open every drawer searching for plastic wrap or duct tape—anything to keep the cloth pressed against the wound. I've already lost too much blood. The lightheadedness tells me that.

I only spare a few minutes to address the gunshot. I don't have any more time to give it. I need a phone. Bracing myself against the counter, I eye the place. It looks like it hasn't been updated since the '80s and I'm praying that means there's a landline somewhere. Every step I take elicits a short groan from the warped floorboards.

There are no photos to go by, nothing to tell me if this is a family home or an old man living alone in this house. It could be a hunting lodge this far out in the woods, but I don't see any guns or trophy mounts. I have no fucking idea. I search the walls of the kitchen then the outlets before coming up empty-handed and moving to the living room. A TV was left on, but no one's there. Someone is in this house; I don't know who and I don't know where, but I know there's someone here. I wish I had my gun on me. I wish I had anything to go by. Anything at all, but I have nothing. It only takes me half a second to see the house phone, complete with a curled-up cord, on what looks like a foldout dinner table next to the worn, brown reclining chair in the back right of the room.

If I had to guess, I'd say an old man lives here. It reminds me of my grandfather's place when I was younger. The foldout dinner tables, the bared shag rug and the faux wood panel walls. Even the off-white color of the ceiling and the scent that lingers. It's from years of smoke.

If I close my eyes a second too long, I can see my pops rocking in the corner chair, smoking a cigar and telling me to keep it down because he can't hear the TV.

For a moment, it's too real. Too lifelike in my mind.

The vision is quickly wiped away at the sound of a toilet being flushed behind me. From the back hall.

The realization is jarring and I hide behind the threshold of the door. My back is pressed against it as the sound of a door opening and closing echoes through the first floor. There's no light in this hall, although it looks like it leads to a garage or maybe a basement. The stairs to the second floor are to the left, back by the dining room.

I pray whoever it is takes their ass upstairs to bed.

I don't have a gun or a weapon; I don't have the energy or strength to defend myself. If my grandfather saw a strange man with a gunshot wound in his house late at night, I can guarantee he wouldn't have asked questions. Shoot first. Or else the other guy might.

I'm as still as can be, barely breathing as I listen to the heavy footsteps. They're slow, giving more evidence that whoever is here is older or at the very least tired.

I listen to him open the fridge, every sound he makes sounding fainter and fainter as I wait with bated breath, feeling the life slowly slip from me.

He grabs whatever he was looking for and goes back into the living room. I'm just behind the wall, so close to the phone, but blocked by his presence.

My mind immediately wanders to Laura and in a helpless moment, I contemplate begging the man to listen and not attack me. I picture myself walking out into the light, hands up in the air, pleading with him to let me use the phone. How would he react to a dying man who snuck into his house?

I don't trust him. I don't trust the situation. I trust no one and if I fail, Laura dies.

I remember every moment I had with her and recalling every second I took advantage of her destroys me, warping my mind and my emotions.

"Hey." The sudden strength in her voice gets my attention. She's been quiet all this week. She doesn't speak but sometimes she cries, like something's just reminded her that she's all alone. Regardless of the fact that I'm there, walking her both ways, holding her hand when she needs it.

I get it. It's the way we mourn. We're fine for moments and then we fall victim to the memories. It kills us to come back to the present.

Even though it's only early November, the bite of winter is in the air and it's turned Laura's neck pink. The tip of her nose is the same shade. With her hand on her front door, keeping it open, she looks out at me.

A gust of wind goes by and I slip my right hand into my jacket pocket, so very aware of how cold the left one is. My palm is warm from her skin and her touch, but the back of my hand is freezing. She let me hold her hand though, so there's no chance I'm letting her go.

"Yeah?" I ask her, raising my voice as I turn on the uneven stone steps of this old townhouse. I think she's going to say thank you;

she says it every day even though she doesn't want me to be her babysitter. At least that's what she says, but I don't believe it. "You already told me thanks," *I remind her before she can say anything.*

She's busy chewing on her bottom lip, her baby blues wide while I wait.

There's a moment, a vulnerable one between us. A moment where she wants something—needs something from me—and I'll be damned if I don't need it too.

This is all up to her though. Every move is hers to make.

"What do you want, Babygirl?" *I ask her, doing everything I can to hide what I want from creeping into my tone.*

The moment is over, waning slowly when she shakes her head, her long hair falling down the front of her sweater and hiding half her face from me. "Never mind. It's nothing."

I shouldn't feel hollow inside when I force the smile to my lips. It matches the one she gives me too.

"Thanks again."

"No problem." *I nearly walk away. I'm so close to letting her shut me out, but just the thought of it makes me feel empty. I don't like the way I feel without her.*

"Hey," *I call back before I can stop myself.*

"Yeah?" *The way she says the single word sounds faint and it almost gets lost in the wind. She perks up with hope though and whatever it is she's hoping for, I hope she gets it.*

"Do you eat?"

It takes her a moment, but she laughs at the ridiculous

question and the sweet sound makes me smile as I jog up the steps to get back to her. "I'm hungry and I was thinking, if you're hungry, you want to come with me?"

I can't be so out of shape that I'm breathless after making my way up her steps to be closer to her but I blame it on that, and not on the nerves. "Come with me to dinner," I say, making it a demand rather than a question.

She chews on that bottom lip for a moment longer, debating as the blush rises to her cheeks. "Yeah," she answers. "I could eat something."

All that tension melts, all the nerves go away. When she's next to me, it's all just fine. It's perfect.

The click of the television and the silence that follows brings me back to now, back to the chance to make things right. *Just a little longer*, I think. He's got to be going to bed.

The stairs creak and with the old floors, I can easily hear him upstairs when he finally leaves. Thank fuck.

I should wait to call Jase, wait until I'm sure that the man upstairs is asleep and won't come back, but my patience is thin. I've already wasted too much time. At that thought, I move as quickly as I can.

I know Jase's phone number by heart so I dial it, holding my breath. I'm fucked if he doesn't answer. And Laura...

Fuck.

The other end only rings twice. Both times, I stare down at my hands as they shake.

"Who's this?" Jase answers in a deadly tone. It's the best thing I've ever heard in my life.

Please God, don't let me be too late. She needs me. She's always needed me.

I need her more. More than anything.

Chapter 5

Laura

My hands are still trembling. I'm huddled up, tucked away in the corner of this bed, bracing myself against the painted white cement wall of the cell. Hours have passed, but I still struggle to fully wrap my head around it all.

I'm a nurse. I've read about it. I comprehend the words. I just can't believe it's true.

Arrhythmia is apparently the least of my worries. The walls of my heart are weak.

Too weak. Even if I'd had my medicine, it wouldn't have helped. It was only a matter of time before my heart gave out.

That's what the doctor said when I woke up in the medical center at the back of the jail. I was out for hours; the defibrillator brought my heart back to a steady beat. I know about the medical center here, but I'm not familiar with the doctor who monitored me. He showed me everything though. I saw my charts.

I have systolic heart failure.

The doctor's voice won't shut up in my head. He keeps looking at me with those pale green eyes from behind his spectacles. *You have systolic heart failure.* His voice was so calm, his hand resting lightly on mine. He was a kind doctor, but as I wiped away the tears from the corners of my eyes, I couldn't help but hate him for having to deliver that news to me.

"Your heart is weak," he told me. *"You'll be high on the donor list; you're in good health."* He touched my shoulder, barely gripping me but I could only look at where his hand met the orange fabric of my newly appointed attire.

The scene plays again and again. It can't be real.

More tests need to be done and an appointment has been scheduled for the first of said tests, but the chest X-ray is a smoking gun. The second I saw it, I knew. He didn't even have to tell me; I knew just from looking.

"The arrhythmia has developed into something more dangerous."

I read all about this in textbooks when I was still in school. I've never had a patient with heart failure though. They're always older in the educational videos and on TV shows.

I'm in my twenties, relatively healthy, but my heart is failing me. Really, I've failed my heart. I knew something was wrong, yet I never followed through. I let my health slip. They could have caught this sooner.

The next appointment, once my current situation is more concrete either way, will consist of an EKG to confirm, and then I wait. I wait for someone to die so I can have their heart. That's the best option I have. Of course, there's medication to take and lifestyle adjustments to relieve the symptoms in the meantime... like removing stressors from my environment. There is no doubt though from Dr. Conway. I won't survive more than a year with this heart. That's what he told me. No more than a year at best.

I hardly notice the hot tears anymore.

Sitting cross-legged on the thin mattress in my new cell, I try to focus on all the other noise around me. At least I have a mattress now, and not just a bench. I have a blanket too, and a toilet identical to the one from before is in the corner.

I don't know if this bed is mine or if the one across from me was supposed to be mine. I'm the only one in this cell, for now. I was told several things while I went through the booking process. But it was all a blur as they took my fingerprints and mug shot. All I kept hearing was: *a year, at most.*

Clank, clank, clank, clank. Someone runs something down the bars of their cell. It came from the right and a bit of a ways down the much wider hall than the one in the holding area. There have to be twenty cells on each side of this wing. A guard tells whoever's making noise to quit it. The voice comes from a man and it reminds me where I am, bringing me back to the present.

In two days, my life has changed to be unrecognizable.

A few inmates hooted and made a ruckus when I was blindly led back here. I didn't pay attention to a thing. Not to where we were going. I hardly remember the sound the bars made as they were closing shut. Even the horrid beep of the lock is less than memorable.

They put me in here and I find it hard to care, but a piece of me does. A piece of me wants out and still has hope; the rest of me can't believe this is real. *Maybe it's shock.* I nod at the thought.

I want to wake up from this nightmare. From the moment Seth told me he killed my father, to the attack and murders in my apartment, to the doctor telling me, *"It's not a death sentence to be on the donor list."*

There are other options but they're risky, and even worse, temporary. He worries the walls of my heart are just too thin for surgery, but that's what second opinions are for. I keep hoping he's wrong. I keep hoping I'm wrong. This can't be real.

My head feels heavy so I let it fall, pushing my hair up as I lean against the cinder block wall. It's suddenly bitterly cold and it takes everything in me to keep it together.

One breath at a time is all I need. *Breathe in*, my heart thumps, *breathe out*, it ticks too quickly this time.

The jarring sound of the bars to my cell dragging open

with a heavy creak causes my eyes to widen.

I don't recognize the guard. He's got to be in his late thirties, at youngest. His jaw is covered with a five o'clock shadow and his cheeks are hollow from his age. They match the wrinkles around his eyes. There are too many guards working in this place for me to tell them apart.

"This is your stop," he speaks and oddly enough, it seems like he meant the words for me. He stands there, his back straight as a rod as a woman wearing orange clothes that match my own, walks into the cell. He never looks at me, even though I stare at him. His embroidered tag reads Brown, I think. It certainly starts with a B.

I don't like that he, just like Walters, doesn't look at me. Or when they do, it's with an air of righteousness. It's possible I've made it up in my mind, but I hate it. I shouldn't be here. The thought desperately tries to turn into spoken words.

Instead of speaking, I drop my gaze, picking at an oddly thick thread in the blanket and waiting for the bars to shut.

It doesn't matter what he or anyone else thinks of me; none of this matters. Still, I want him to know I didn't do it. There's an itch in the back of my throat and a cold tingle that dances along my skin, giving me goosebumps, at the mere suggestion that he thinks I'm guilty.

I didn't do anything wrong. The small piece of me that's focused on getting out screams in my head even though it sounds like a whimper caught at the back of my tongue.

The larger part of me knows it doesn't matter. Where I'm sitting doesn't matter. I have no intention of moving if I can help it.

All that matters is that I don't miss my next visit to the doctor and schedule with another to get a second opinion. To find out whether the bespectacled doctor's diagnosis is correct. And whether or not I qualify for the donor list, like he said I did. That's what matters.

A rough ball scratches its way down my throat as I swallow thickly, finally looking at my companion. She takes her time walking to the other bed, pushing up the orange sleeves as she does. Black ink scrolls its way down her arms. It's a scripture of some sort but it's no longer sharp, it's faded and fuzzy from years of being on her skin. She blows a stray strand of hair out of her face.

Years of being conditioned to be polite and uphold formalities wins out. "I'm Laura," I tell her even though her back is to me as she smooths the mattress sheet. Although I'm sitting, I know she's taller than me, broader than me. Big-boned is an expression my grandma would have used to describe her. She carries a lot of weight, but it looks like she works out just the same. Her black hair is lifted off her neck in a ponytail that's not smooth at all. It's like she haphazardly pulled it up. I suppose to her, what hairstyle she chooses doesn't matter. I get that.

The bed creaks and squeaks as she climbs onto it with

a bit of a bounce that comes with aggression, mirroring my position and leaning against the wall.

She crosses her arms while she talks. "I know who you are."

Thud, my instincts recognize that tone. It's a warning cadence, a deathly low one that's meant to strike fear. I've heard it plenty in the old bar I used to work at, the Club, and plenty on the streets. Instead of eliciting fear as it's intended, irritation flashes through me. A match is lit and it gracefully falls to a line of fuel, igniting its way through me.

How fucking dare she? I deserve to at least revel in my pity party. *How fucking dare she?*

It's then I see just how much muscle she has. Although I keep my expression calm and I don't hint in the slightest at the terror I know she wants to evoke, I size her up. Every inch of her.

"Oh," I say sweetly, "the guard didn't tell me your name." I smile naively at the bitch, staring into her deep brown eyes. Shrugging, I do my best to look pathetic. I'm sure with my red-rimmed eyes and tearstained cheeks, it's not hard to appear otherwise.

I'm ice cold down to the marrow of my bones when she hisses in a breath, "Damn, you'll be a hard one." She shakes her head gently, that hair behind her head swaying as she does, as if she truly has remorse. The chill in my blood pricks harshly, sending a bite of frost to cover every inch of me. "You seem sweet."

I let my lips part and feign confusion. The dumbass eats it up, leaning forward with an expression that tells me she's oh so sad to inform me. "I'm waiting on a note," she says.

"A note?"

"Telling me whether or not to kill you," she says and I let my eyes widen, halting my breath. As if I didn't know she was here to hurt me. *Kill me?* That part is new. Why, I don't know. This could all be a joke, a ruse. I don't give a fuck.

She might know my name, but she doesn't know who I am. She doesn't know where I came from. My hackles rise inside and an angry girl I'm far too familiar with emerges.

I swallow and then quicken my breath, letting her feel what she wants. My fear, my turmoil. "I didn't do any—"

She cuts me off, not letting my plea go on; thank fuck for that.

"I know. It's unfortunate," she says and tosses her head back. "I'm a killer for hire in here," she confesses. I stare wide eyed and think about Seth, about my father, about my fucked-up heart, all in order to bring tears to swell in my eyes. Outwardly I'm fragile, stricken with her confession. Internally, I imagine this woman killing inmates and getting away with it. *Calling them sweet.*

I let my gaze fall to the ink on her arm. Tally marks and trophies. My eyes whip back up to hers when she speaks.

"I don't want to do it, sweetie," she tells me and I make a mental note that when I kill her, I'll make sure to call her *sweetie*. A side of me I barely know anymore emerges. The side that kept a baseball bat at my front door and a pocketknife in every drawer of my home. A side that hates more than it loves, a side that doesn't have hope, because it doesn't want it.

"I see," I say softly, sniffling and wiping under my eyes, even though enough tears haven't gathered to actually fall. "A note?" I question, prying for more information.

"They said it'll be quick if Marcus gives the word. Sorry this is happening."

The mention of Marcus causes true fear to trickle in, but it's tainted, stained by hate that anyone thinks they can kill me. I've never heard of Marcus killing a woman. Never. That fact alone makes me think she's lying. Not about what's to come, but about who's behind it. Or maybe I just have too much faith in the faceless man I've read all about in those notebooks.

"Give me a smoke, will ya?" the woman asks as my mind wanders and a deep crease settles in my forehead before I notice the fingers reaching into the bars. A guard hands her a smoke and she gingerly accepts it, climbing off the bed and telling the guard thanks. Pulling a lighter from her pocket, she leans against the wall, flicking the small lighter back and forth as the tip of the cigarette turns a bright orange and she breathes in then blows out a billow of smoke.

"I didn't think you could have lighters in here," I barely speak, looking over her tattoos again on her inner forearm. I know them, I've seen them on psych patients before. They're gang tats and the ones on her right forearm are credits for kills. I only got a glance but there are at least twenty.

"You can't have lighters in here," she answers as she plays with the lighter she has in her hand. Shrugging, she continues. "You can't ask for a smoke and just get it. You can't have this either," she says and pulls a blade from her pocket. It's a simple pocketknife, with a corkscrew at the end and she taps it against her temple. "The blade is cleaner but takes too long. The corkscrew is more efficient. Bloodier, but more efficient because of the size of the wound."

Another guard passes and all the while, she has the knife out and a smoke in her hand. She takes a puff and blows the smoke my way.

"Why do they let you?" I ask and try to play up the naivety.

"Because we're all on the same payroll, working for the same higher command. Well, some of them... others, I pay off. I get paid to kill and I pay them to help me." She shrugs, taking another long inhale. "This shift is full of people who'll look the other way for the right price. It's that easy."

My breathing is shallow, my vision black around the edges. She's not fucking with me, she's truly going to kill me and the people in here will let her.

The true fear is back, but so much anger comes with the knowledge.

"I really am sorry."

She talks to me like it's a given. As if I'm easy prey.

It's her. And me.

I nod, my lips still parted in feigned disbelief and then the woman lies back, not even looking at me.

I bring my knees into my chest so I can bury my head in them. I keep my eyes on her though. She can't see my expression. She can't see the unbridled hate.

Every footstep beyond the bars steals my attention.

She's waiting on a note. I need to get that note first.

Chapter 6

Seth

Their graves were right next to each other. Side by side. I knew mine would be the third. The plot was empty and I knew I'd be buried there. My grandfather, my father, and then me. My grandfather was a stubborn old man, set in his ways and vocal about them.

I never liked him much. You can't ever like someone if you fear them the way I feared him. He died when I was young and as I stood there tracing the etching on his stone, I wondered if I'd feel the same way had I gotten to know him when I was older. After all, I feared my father, but I loved him. I hated him sometimes, but I respected and loved him. I understood. Children can't understand this life and I stood there thinking, that must have been why I didn't like my grandfather.

"You all right?" A small feminine voice broke through the hiss of the wind. Laura clutched her coat around her and I opened my arms so she could take refuge there.

"Fine."

"Then why are you here?" she questioned. Her no-nonsense bluntness always made me smile, even that day. With the bite of the cold nipping my nose, I sniffed and then shrugged. "I can't just come visit my pops?" I asked her, although it was rhetorical.

She peeked up at me through her thick lashes and said, "Please, Seth. Tell me what's wrong."

So much was wrong. She couldn't do anything to change it and she shouldn't have had to deal with that shit just because she was with me. I'd never make her take on my burdens.

"I was just thinking of my grandfather, that's all. I promise." I offered her a small smile, which she reluctantly returned and when she did, I kissed the crown of her head.

She leaned in closer to me, taking her hand from her pocket, wrapping her arm around my waist and she slipped that hand into my coat pocket. I liked the move. Even more, I liked that she'd been making them more readily. She wasn't holding back anymore. I don't know what changed, but she wasn't trying to run anymore. I had her. She really wasn't going to leave me, at least that's what I thought.

"You know you can tell me anything, right?" she asked me in a whisper. Her cheek was pressed against my chest and when

another sharp gust blew by, she didn't complain. She stood there by my side, quiet and ready to wait longer if I wanted.

"I know," I told her although it was a lie. I could never tell her everything. There were some things she would never know if I could help it.

"Can I tell you anything?" she asked, and a hint of insecurity revealed itself in her tone.

Resting my chin on the top of her head I told her easily, "Of course." Although nervousness crept in, not knowing what she would say.

"I love you, Seth, and I'm afraid you're going to break my heart."

I thought I came there to that grave to pray that when I died, I wouldn't be buried next to them. That I'd be buried somewhere else, somewhere with a different kind of family. Instead I stood there praying that I'd never break her heart. It was the only good thing I'd ever have. I couldn't break it. I'd never forgive myself.

"If I ever break your heart," I told her honestly, "I'll never forgive myself."

My eyes barely stay open as the memory from almost a decade ago leaves me. My lids are heavy, but I fight it. I know I'm lying down; I can see the ceiling and fan blades whipping around. The light is bright and right above my head.

I'm hot, so fucking hot. But more than that, I can't keep my eyes open. I fight it, willing my body to obey me.

It takes only a few seconds to see the IV stand, to feel the prick in my arm of a needle, to sense there are people around me.

"Stop drugging me," I say and pull at the tube in my arm chaotically. *Get it out. Get it out.* The need to run is strong but I don't remember why. The needle slips out but not fully, and the hot blood in the crook of my arm spurs me further, ripping pain through my forearm as I hiss, rolling over on the sofa although strong arms keep me down.

My hands wrap around forearms, trying to shove them away. My muscles coil and a new pain shoots up my right side. Before I can kick my feet up, someone yells, "Get him," and pins my lower half down.

"Fuck," a man curses under his breath. It's strained and it takes me a moment to recognize it's Jase. "You need the fluids," Jase grits out.

My back presses into the cushions beneath me as the hands holding me down shove harder even though I stopped struggling.

"Stay down," he orders and I don't have the strength to answer. My head spins. It's hot and bright.

"What happened?" I ask and my voice sounds far away. I'm trying to remember. Nothing is coming to me though.

"You were passed out when we got there. Scared the shit out of the old man."

"The old man?" What's the last thing I remember? My face is hot. *The fight.* She threw something at me. Laura... she punched me. Her eyes are filled with pain in my memory. I shake it away. No, no, that didn't happen.

"What happened?" I question again, sounding delirious even to my own ears.

"You lost a lot of blood from the shot," Jase says calmly and then he tells me to hold still. A random detail comes to me, the prick reminding me of another.

"They gave me something."

"Stay still," he warns again and more of what happened plays in my mind. It comes in flickers. Black and white slides of what happened as the needle pierces my forearm, finding a new vein. My jaw hardens, tightening and I refuse to react as everything comes flooding back.

"Laura," I finally speak, the room starting to settle. "They're going to kill her."

"We know. You told us. This isn't the first time you've woken up like this."

"They said they'd kill her!" The words rush from me, my breathing coming in ragged as I remember what he said. *Make it quick.*

Jase doesn't respond and dread spreads through me. "I don't need anything," I speak as I try to sit up but Jase is there to push me back down. The force of his shove knocks my breath from me. My head is still spinning.

"You need fluids." His voice is harsh and although somewhere deep down I wonder if he's right, I deny it, shaking my head and telling him to fuck off.

"Two hours," he tells me like that will keep me down.

"Just two hours." The second time he speaks it's like he's asking me.

"She may not have two hours," I say and my voice breaks. The words splinter with the lack of hope. "They're going to kill her because of me." I remember something important suddenly and speak again before Jase can say anything.

"Steven Davis. Find him, kill him." I remember the name. I remember that dumb fuck. "He's the one who said it. He's one of Marcus's—"

"You told us last night. We already found him, found the lot of them."

The lot of them? I don't remember. I struggle to recall the details.

"You said there were four and there were. The van was at the docks, looks like they were waiting on someone. Don't think they expected us to show up, but we had the trace on Davis still."

"You got them?" I want them all dead. Every one of them needs to die.

"They took off and he had a gun." Jase talks to me absently and I look between him and the thin curtains over the windows. I recognize the bay windows, the coffee table, the art on the walls. It's his girlfriend Bethany's house. It was probably closer than the bar for him to transport me from wherever I was. More importantly, it's dark outside. Everything comes back, drip by drip.

Jase keeps talking as I remember the pieces of what happened. "We had to shoot. We got him, he gave us the other three before he bled out and Declan got the plates on their vehicle. We've got their names and Declan has possible locations."

"Let me, let me go." I struggle to sit up.

"Just two hours," he says and then I remember how he said *last night*.

"What time is it?" I ask, my blood pounding in my ears. How much time has passed? All three of them will pay but first, I need her safe. I need Laura back and by my side. "Is she okay?"

"Eight. We didn't get you until four this morning. And yes, we have eyes on her."

My hand travels down my side and my fingers brush over stitches. Everything moves slowly as I get colder and colder. Too much time has passed. "Where is she?" I question and again Jase doesn't answer.

"We need to get to her!" I rip out the IV again and this time I have more strength, more alertness so when Jase's arm comes down I'm prepared with my forearm already braced and shoving back. Whoever's at my feet got a good kick to his groin and I'm up and off the sofa, breathing heavily like a wild animal and staring at a pissed off Jase Cross and some poor guy who's doubled over.

The doc, maybe. I don't know. I don't recognize him or

his voice.

"Don't be stupid," Jase says lowly, taking a step forward but not reaching for me.

"Fuck, shit," the man I kicked sputters. I got him hard and if I wasn't so concerned about Laura, maybe I'd care.

"We have guys on the inside." Jase barely acknowledges the man. His focus stays on me.

"Who?" I say and the word comes out deep, rougher and louder than I intended. The man I don't know slowly rises, his face both flushed and scrunched like he's trying to hide his pain. "Sorry," I bite out when he looks at me with contempt. He doesn't respond but I can hear him swallow from all the way over here. Judging by where his hands are and the fact they don't move even as he walks out of the living room and toward the half bath that's down the hall, I hit him where it hurts.

Remorse courses slowly through me as my vision becomes clearer and the pieces of what's happened line up, one after the other.

"A few guards are keeping an eye out. Walters, for one. Williams and Shultz. Chris Mowers."

"Who's getting her out?" I question, hating how tight my throat is at the thought of her in a cell. She's not meant to be there.

"She shouldn't even be in there," I add before Jase can say anything and both of my hands fly to the back of my head.

My breathing is quick, too quick as I pace in front of him.

It's dark in this living room, but the floors sound the same as they did before. The soft groan of old hardwood. I look Jase in the eyes, pausing my steps and noting how tired he looks, how his five o'clock shadow is far too long. "It should've been me," I say, dragging out the confession from the back of my throat.

A different kind of pain washes through me and I close my eyes, remembering how she shut the window even knowing the cops were coming.

"She took the fall and it should have been me." Shit, everything would be different if she hadn't done that. She'd be safe. "She shouldn't be in there!"

"Listen to me," Jase says in a hushed tone and he sounds closer. I open my eyes slowly and he is, he's right next to me, reaching out his hand and gripping my shoulder. "She's going to be fine."

"You didn't hear him," I start to say, my head shaking chaotically as I remember the voice in the woods, the dead fucker who said, *make it quick*. I'll never get it out of my memory. I won't be able to sleep without hearing Davis again and again the moment my eyes close. Not until I know for certain Laura is safe.

"That prick is dead," he says and Jase's tone is firm, but it doesn't matter.

"The prick works for *Marcus*," I stress, hating that I have to justify my concern to him. He should know I can't sit back.

He should fucking know.

"He's never done anything like this. He's never come after a woman." Jase's voice is calm with his head shaking just slightly. The small, rhythmic movements are at odds with my own. He repeats, "He's never come after a woman."

My heart thuds. It's not good enough. I can't sit back hoping Marcus doesn't give the word and that the men on the inside are able to prevent anything bad from happening to her.

She's mine to protect. She needs me.

"I can't sit back," I say and my voice cracks on the last word as I close my eyes, moving my fisted hands to the crown of my head. I'm barely steady, but I'm capable of seeing her there. Watching her pace around a cell she doesn't belong in. Watching her walk alone when I should be there for putting her through it all. "I have to see her."

"Visiting hours are over," Jase speaks as if that's the end of it. Hate is brutal, coursing its way through me. I've never resented the man, but what I feel for him at this moment borders on unforgivable.

When I open my eyes, doing my best to keep from uttering the spew of curses that choke me, I see a jacket draped over the sofa arm, probably Jase's, and on top of it are his keys.

He's not my boss anymore. And he sure as fuck isn't a friend. He'll have to kill me to keep me away from her.

"My car still at her place?" I ask him casually. My gaze doesn't move from the glint of silver metal until he says, "We got it. It's out front. Your wallet and phone were in the van at the docks."

"Where are my keys?" I question him.

He doesn't respond verbally. Instead he motions with his arm behind me and lets it fall to his side.

I don't waste a second putting my wallet in my back pocket, my phone in the front and then snatch my keys from the end table to the right of the sofa.

"You're just going to leave?" he says, raising his voice as I make my way to the door. With my back to him, I pause.

"Bethany stitched you up, by the way. We had to come here to get everything she needed. She risked her job to get the meds."

Glancing over my shoulder at him, I tell him, "Thanks. I'll tell her thanks when I see her again."

"You just kicked her boss in the nuts. You may want to apologize at some point." He's resigned in his tone, but there's a hint of friendliness. He huffs in humor and bends down to grab his own keys and then his jacket.

"You have to know I can't just sit here."

"I do," he admits and then he adds, "Don't do anything stupid, Seth."

He doesn't look at me and he doesn't wait for a response. Instead he pulls out his phone and dials someone. I don't wait to hear who.

The pain is a dull white noise running through me. The

adrenaline outweighs any and everything that could keep me down.

I'm not conscious of what I'm doing when I get in the car. The headlights are the only bit of light in the neighborhood, but the streets have a few cars scattered through them. I'm careful as I drive, recounting everything that happened. Making sure I know all of it.

My memory stutters at the pain in her eyes when I told her the truth about how her father died. Everything else is red. Blood colors and stains every moment.

A section of road on the way to the jail is nearly black from the lack of streetlights on this side of town, and there are hardly any cars out here. It gets dark early this time of year.

The bank is lit up though. It's a beacon in the night. Every window is brightly lit. I know it's closed. It closes at six every day and it's closed all day on Sundays. Everything around here closes at six except for the bars and the church.

I'm not even thinking; my gaze doesn't stray from the front of the bank. It's mostly glass. I know I'm conscious of that. Glass is easy to drive through.

My foot feels heavy on the gas and the rev of the engine sends a thrum of anticipation to my veins. I'm hot as I turn the wheel just slightly. Just enough to put the bank in my path.

Visiting hours are over. Jase's words echo in my head. We can't get in to the jail without signing in. I'm sure he thinks she's safe and that she'll still be there tomorrow, but I can't risk it. I won't. He has the distance to be logical, to allow the risks. I don't have that luxury.

My heart races as I keep my hands steady on the wheel, bracing myself.

If they won't let me visit her or see her right now, then I'll join her.

They can arrest me for attempted robbery, for... I don't fucking know what and I don't care. Either way, I'll get to see her. I just need to get through those doors one way or the other.

My foot slams down to the floorboard of the car. The lights blur in front of me and my muscles tighten, ready for the impact.

The shatter of glass and jolt of the tires meeting stone don't mean anything to me.

None of it matters.

The airbag goes off and slams against my face. My neck whips back, unprepared.

It's barely anything. I've taken worse hits.

None of this shit matters, I think as I wait, letting the bag deflate, listening to the screeching of the alarms and then within minutes, sirens.

Arrest me, charge me, lock me up.

I pull my phone out of my pocket and text Jase: *Just get me close enough to protect Laura.*

The ringtone goes off within a few seconds. He's calling but I put my phone back in my pocket, ignoring him as the sirens get louder.

Chapter 7

Laura

"What about any brothers? Or sisters?" the woman asks conversationally. She finally told me her name is Jean. No last name, just Jean.

I have to swallow before I can answer, since my throat is dry from answering all her questions. Back-to-back she wants to know pointless details. Occasionally there's a bout of silence, but I hate that even more. I can't decide if she's sadistic and wants to know particulars of my life before she ends it, or if she's trying to befriend me as justification to her own conscience that she's not a bad person and is just following orders.

"None. You?" I ask back. I've done this a few times, asking the same question in return. It's mostly out of habit but Jean only shakes her head, either refusing to answer, or simply saying no. I'm not sure which. She could have a dozen brothers out there and still she shakes her head like she's done every other time I've turned the question back on her.

I don't know shit about her but now she knows all about where I grew up, what I do for a living, why I chose the East Coast. Mundane questions that amount to nothing more than small talk. I think it's a bit tedious considering I hate her fucking guts.

Everything I told her was true, except for what happened yesterday. She got half the truth and half the lie I gave Officer Walsh. Just in case she knows about Seth, I told her I'm involved with him. I told her he took off yesterday after we got into a fight and that made her laugh. A deep guttural laugh that brought a genuine smile to her face. She's missing two teeth, in the back upper right of her mouth. I've gotten a good view of her smile a few times now.

Again she shakes her head, refusing to answer and lies back down, stretching easily, as if she doesn't have a worry in the world.

I haven't moved in the hours we've been sitting in here. My muscles are tense, every single one and my back feels stiff. Jean, on the other hand, moves easily in our cell. I haven't taken my eyes off of her while she looks anywhere but at me for the most part. She has a habit of tapping the back of her knuckles against the bars of the locked cell when she's thinking. I assume she's thinking about something. She could simply be waiting for that note to float by.

I hate her. I hate everything about her. As time passes, the hate only seeps deeper and deeper into my psyche. I've imagined rolling up the bedsheet, slipping it around her throat and choking her. She's taller than me, so I wouldn't be able to do it when she's standing.

It's not quite practical, but the image of it happening has ingrained itself in me.

She's stronger than me, so slamming her head into the toilet wouldn't work. And the toilet itself is similar to one on an airplane—there's no standing water. So I can't drown the bitch.

I want to ask her how many people she's killed and how she's done it. Simply to justify the obsessive and hateful thoughts that suffocate me, but a girl who's frightened wouldn't do that. I've done everything I can to make sure she thinks I'm terrified. I've even begged her to spare my life. I've brought on tears.

I'll act for as long as I have to, until one of these plots in my head becomes feasible.

A contented sigh leaves Jean as she lays her head back, staring at the ceiling but then closing her eyes as if she'll nap. It has to be late now. Lights out was called a bit ago and this floor went dark in an instant, making my heart race for a moment until my sight had adjusted. It seems like lights out would be a good time for something like a hit to go down.

Nothing happened though. Nothing has happened since she walked in here. Only question after pointless question.

The squeak of a cart rolling down the hall rips Jean's eyes wide open. She props her head up with her forearms crossed above her, still lying on her back but other than that movement, she remains still.

Thump, thump, my heart is steady, but fast until the cart comes into view. It's a simple silver, three-shelved cart. That's when my beating organ falls down to the pit of my stomach. I swear I can feel it beating there. The nurse rolling it by doesn't stop, doesn't say anything; she doesn't even look our way. I barely even get a look at her. It's dark and her straight hair is black. She doesn't turn to us and doesn't come close to the cell. Jean sure as hell was alert though. I suppose now I know how she'll be receiving her note. It makes me sick thinking about it and waiting around.

Even when the nurse is gone, the thumping still feels far lower than it should be.

"Don't worry," she says and her tone steals my attention and she smiles grimly. "When it comes, I'll make it so fast you won't have time to wonder if what I'm given is the note, or another smoke." She says it so easily. Like it's a kindness and not a threat to instill uncertainty and fear.

Jean cracks her neck and then rolls over, facing me even though her eyes are closed. Time ticks by and still, I don't move. I don't know how much longer I can go without sleeping. My eyes are heavy and dry. They've never been this raw in my life. How could I possibly sleep though?

I could close my eyes, and never wake up again.

I don't know if she's feigning sleep or if she's really capable of dozing off right now. More time passes. Sleep threatens to take me and when I try to adjust my right leg, the idea of lying down and giving in seems so... alluring. As if my body could rest even if I stay awake.

I can't go to sleep, but I have to. Maybe I could scream and beg for them to let me out of here. I could tell the guards she's trying to kill me. Although she said if I did, she'd kill me regardless of whether or not she was given a note. If she's sleeping though, maybe she wouldn't hear.

With my hand over my eyes, I focus on breathing. I don't know what else I can do. I can't sleep, so I can only think about begging to be let out of here and risk calling her bluff. I hate feeling like a victim, but I've been backed into a corner with no way out.

Movement from the right, behind the bars, steals every ounce of focus I have left.

I recognize the guard, the one who was watching me when I was in holding. Walters. My gaze darts between him and Jean as he makes his way toward the cell. He's walking toward me silently, not yet in view for Jean. I could ask him for help. I could beg him even, but there's something about him, something that keeps me silent.

His eyes reach mine when I look back at him after noting that Jean really does look like she's asleep, and he holds them for only a moment before dropping to his knee right in front of our cell. From here I can see him clearly; Jean wouldn't be able to even if her eyes were open and she was waiting for him. He's opposite me and not her.

I question if he's the one who would give her the note and an animal inside of me screams in agony. He could have just killed me then. If he knew, why make me wait? There's a piece that doesn't fit, though. Walters lets me see him. He waited for Jean to be sleeping.

Again Walters looks up at me and I stare back, watching him place something just under the bars. He scoots it back, giving it a small quiet toss so it's closer to the toilet in the corner of the cell.

With a small nod, he rises and stalks off, back the way he came. Jean never would have seen him. Whatever he left there, it's meant for me.

My eyes turn back to Jean's closed ones. She didn't hear him, didn't see him either.

The tension that's been building in my stomach rises. It takes over my entire body until I feel like I'm trembling although I'm eerily still. I watch her for too long, knowing I need to get to it first. I need to see what it is.

There's a feeling inside sometimes that urges you. It knows this moment will change everything.

The visceral reaction that takes hold when I slowly stand, giving Jean a tight smile as she peers at me through narrowed slits, is overwhelming.

The knots in my stomach nearly make me throw up. A cold sweat lines my skin and I pray the bitch can't see it.

"Just have to pee," I mutter and swallow thickly. *Please don't see. Please don't watch me.*

"Don't be nervous, sweetie," she says, giving me that pet name again but the spike of anger is nothing compared to the fear. This moment is decisive. I know it. Every part of me knows it. From the sweat on my skin to the very soul that'll leave me if Jean gets that package first.

My lips quiver as I huff and I try to play it off like I'm nervous about her watching me pee and nothing else. She watches me though, following me as I walk in the small space that separates our beds and stalk to the only toilet just feet from where she's lying.

My heart sputters. *Don't look down*, I pray. *Don't let her look to the floor.*

I'm still wearing my sneakers and in the few seconds it takes to get to where I'm headed, I debate on stepping on whatever it is in order to hide it. I don't know what's inside. I don't know if it'll make a noise that will clue her in. So I don't do it. I stand there, knowing it's by my feet and meet her gaze as my thumbs slip into the elastic waistband of the pants they gave me.

The beats are so fast in my chest, I feel faint.

"A little..." I barely get out the words, taking a long, unwanted blink. Now is not the time, but I can barely focus.

"Privacy?" Jean says and huffs a laugh and actually smiles. I can see the glimmer of her grin as she rolls back onto her side. "Make it fast," she orders.

I drop my pants quickly, just in case she looks and sit there, forcing a dribble of pee to leave me. It's only when I reach down, feeling my entire body turn to ice and grab the package with both hands that I'm able to release myself. I unwrap the package while I do and there's no note, not a damn thing but a sliver of metal. It's thin, very thin.

It looks almost like an arrowhead, with a very small handle that doesn't hurt to hold, but the edges of it are sharp. After wiping myself, I test its strength. Whatever metal it is, it's strong as hell.

A shiv. The package I was given, is a shiv.

They want me to kill her first. Seth? The Cross brothers? Someone aimed to help me. Or rather, to help me save myself.

Heat replaces the cold as I stand up, securing the piece in my palm from her sight. The wrapping is easily disposed of with the toilet paper and I stand on shaky legs, staring at her still form.

I was meant to kill her. I knew that the first moment she spoke. It's one thing to know. One thing to think about it. To daydream about bashing her head into the wall.

It's another entirely to do it.

It's like having an out-of-body experience; as though I'm only watching as I take the four strides. *One.* Tick. *Two.* My shoes are heavy. *Three.* That lightness is no longer there. *Four.* My body screams to do it. Adrenaline surges through my body. It's a kill or be killed situation.

I think it's the shadow of my body over her eyes that cues her to look at me. And that's exactly what she's doing when I bring the shiv to her throat with a single slash. The blood sprays down her body and I nearly do it again, but it's not necessary. I would have done it over and over to ensure she didn't get up from that bed ever again. But I don't have to. Once was enough.

Whatever word she was going to say doesn't escape.

The hate in her eyes vanishes and it's replaced with absolute shock, then terror.

She doesn't reach out for me. Instead she grabs her throat with both hands as if she could stop it. She tries to keep the blood in as it gushes out.

The puncture was deep. I'm a nurse. It was more than deep enough to do its job.

She's able to back away from the edge of the small bunk, her legs kicking out to push her into the corner. Her eyes are wide, her pupils dilated as she stares at me all the while.

I don't realize I'm crying until she goes still.

Relief is not something I feel. It's another feeling,

although not guilt. Hopelessness maybe. It weighs me down as I reach forward to wipe off the handle of the shiv on her sheets, not disturbing the blood. Her hands have blood on them, but I feel like if she'd sliced her own throat, she would have dropped it before reaching for her throat out of instinct. Having no prints is better for forensics than having a bloody print that doesn't make sense. She wouldn't have tried to stop the bleeding and then reached for the shiv again.

It disturbs me on some level, I note as heat pricks down my skin, that I'm able to think clearly enough.

Until I realize I'm breathing again, my heart is rhythmic.

Fear of dying at her hands is gone. She made the first move. I made the last.

I wait until I rumple my own sheets, making sure I don't have any evidence of blood on me, before I scream, shrill and horrific. I hate myself and what I've become. This version of me who murders so easily. Anyone could do it, though. It didn't take strength or imagination. It only took being pushed. First by her, then a gentle push from Walters.

"Help!" I yell so loud it feels as if my throat is on fire. Sucking in air, I scream again. The lights shine brightly in the entire place. The groans and murmurs from other residents in the neighboring cells are barely heard. Someone tells me to shut up. Another inmate calls me a little bitch.

They don't know. It's only then that I realize I may really have gotten away with it. So long as no one saw.

"What happened here?" a gruff man asks and rips open the cell door, staring wide eyed between the dead girl and then me. At a version of how I truly feel, scared and huddled up in the corner of the bed, covering myself with the thin blanket as if it will save me. It's Guard B. The one who brought her in here.

"She killed herself," I say, letting my voice quiver and try to cry again. When I see her there and the pool of dark red blood that's soaked into the sheets, crying is easy. I don't like that I did it. There's not a damn thing about this that makes me feel anything but agony.

"Oh hell," Guard B mutters. I notice Walters standing just behind the opening to the cell just as Guard B speaks into a walkie-talkie attached to his shirt. He calls for a medic, as if a medic could help her now.

The guard who gave the gift of salvation, Walters, doesn't look at me. He doesn't say a word when the other man says into his speaker to check the security feeds after pronouncing Jean dead. My anxiety would be heightened if Walters had reacted in the least. He simply stands there, unfazed and waiting.

I'm stuck where I am, barely holding on to my sanity as everyone else moves around me. Everyone seems to shift about but no one tells me to move so I stay right where I am and just how I was before Jean was brought in here. It doesn't take long before they decide her death is obviously from a cut to the throat and that she can be moved.

Walters never leaves, but neither does Guard B, whose name is actually Bernard. I finally got a good look at his name tag. It was in between glances at Jean. She's dead. I really killed her.

I can't imagine what you're supposed to feel when you murder another person, but this doesn't feel adequate. I felt more remorse and more guilt when Cami was lying dead at my feet than I do now.

The squeaky metal of a gurney is what I focus on. Tears are too easy to come if I think about Cami. My knuckles are white as I grip the sheets.

"Get her out of here," Walters orders. He gestures for me to get up as the men leave the cell. "I'm taking her in for questioning," he says, addressing the first guard, the one who eyes me suspiciously, Mr. Bernard. The man doesn't protest. He doesn't say anything at all.

He knows. I can feel it in the way he looks at me. I think he knows a lot that goes on around here. He doesn't spend long looking at me, letting his gaze roam up and down my body, in a way I think will give me hives, before turning and leaving.

All of this, all of the moving chess pieces and the lives at stake—I don't want anything to do with it. If I could tell Bernard that, I would. I didn't want to do this. I *had* to.

I'm in far too deep and I didn't ask to be. I've only felt this way one other time. The night death lay on my hands as I cried on the floor. I feel like I'm back there on the other side of the country. I can't stop the visions of Cami and they bring fresh hot tears to my eyes as I stand there, waiting for Walters to stop patting me down.

I'm busy wiping them away, too busy to realize the cell is quiet and only the single guard is in there with me. The feeling of death slipping around me and gripping my ankles is one I haven't felt in so long. It's cold. Death is so cold. He may have given me my way out, but I still don't trust Walters. I don't trust anyone in here.

I stare up at Walters, wondering what would have happened if I'd stayed in California all those years ago. If I'd never run away. Would this have been inevitable? Another life dying in order to save mine... would it have only happened sooner if I'd never run?

"Don't worry about the tapes," the guard whispers although his hands are on his hips and the way he's towering over me is not at all comforting. I have to wipe my nose with my sleeve before I can breathe.

"What?" I say and blink, the constellation of tears in my eyelashes obscuring my view.

"You did good," he tells me and I do everything I can not to noticeably allow what I'm feeling to show on the outside. "I don't think anyone thought you'd kill her. It was just supposed to make you feel protected. But damn, you did good."

Chapter 8

Seth

Seven abrasions are scattered on my right hand and truth be told, I don't know where they're from. There's a large bruise on my wrist with a tinge to it that makes me aware it's not fresh. Not compared to the one I see on my jaw. That bruise came from the crash. I know that much.

I graze the freshest of the cuts with the rough callus on my thumb, letting the pain keep me awake. With all the shit that's gone down in the last forty-eight hours, I don't know what left which of the marks that cover my body. My tongue slips along the crack on the right side of my bottom lip. *Crash.* That one's from the crash too. I can identify some of them at least.

The door opens slowly with an ominous creak, and I wish it were anyone other than this prick. Walsh's back is to me as he silently closes the door. The soft click is the only indication that it's shut. I don't watch him, but I know from the noise that echoes in the small room that he's sitting across the metal table from me. I'm afraid of what I'll do to him if I look at him.

He's in the way. He's choosing to stand in the way of me seeing her. I know how this works; I've played these politics. He could have let me see her, could have put the two of us in a room together with no issues. He's choosing not to. That puts him on my list of people to fuck over the first chance I get.

"I need to see Laura," I say and my voice is hoarse as it fills the tense space between us.

The slap of paperwork that hits the table is greeted with the grinding of my back teeth. It's been hours since I've been arrested. Hours of her being alone and in harm's way. I haven't had a chance to talk to anyone I have on the inside. Not with this fucker hovering.

He needs to get off my dick.

"She was sitting there about..." Walsh pauses and takes in a deep breath, letting time slip by. "About twenty-four hours ago. No," he's quick to correct himself, sounding surer with the "no" than anything else I've heard from him so far. The chair legs beneath him grate on the concrete floor as he leans forward, resting his clasped hands in front of him. That's the only bit of him I dare to look at. "No, it's been almost two days actually since Laura's been brought in."

Forty-eight hours. Two days. A wave of pain hits me from behind my eyes, residual from God knows what and I pinch the bridge of my nose, my eyes closed.

"I'd like to see her," I say, trying to be polite and courteous. It's only a matter of getting out of this fucking room. The second I'm past this stage of questioning, my men will take me to her. They'll find a way. It doesn't matter how.

"A lot's happened." Cody's voice is tight. "She's had a rough few days, hasn't she?"

Sharp pangs of hate stab through me. Lifting my gaze to his, I bite out, "All the more reason I should see her." My throat tightens and anxiousness claws at the back of it. I don't like not knowing. It's the worst feeling in the world, not knowing what's happened.

It's silent for far too long and all I can do is think about her alone in here. In a fucking cell! *Why?* Because of me.

My chest pains are deep and brutal, like my rib cage is closing in on itself. Bracing my hand over my chest, I do my best to keep it all down. "I'll make it right," I say but my voice cracks and I hate myself. The sound of my words betrays me. I didn't mean to say them out loud. They weren't for Walsh. They're for Laura.

Everything was always for her.

How did it get so fucked? How did we get here?

One breath in, and my back straightens. All the heat suffocating me slowly subsides to the cold darkness that keeps me in control. "I'd like to see Laura."

"And I'd like an answer to any of my questions."

My lips part, then close again. He can't play both sides. I thought he'd decided, but maybe this is for show. Maybe there's someone else on the other side of that mirror and he has to be a fucking prick right now.

"You haven't told us anything. You've been mute since you were cuffed." Anger slices through his words. "I don't think you were trying to rob a bank. No one in here does. You deliberately crashed into the front entrance though, the footage shows that."

The rough skin on the pad of my thumb glides over a fresh cut on my other hand. I don't speak. I don't look at him.

"I think you just wanted to see her. Couldn't wait for visiting hours?" Walsh asks and his tone is so damn condescending.

My head lifts slowly until I meet him in the eyes. Dark circles lay under his tired icy gaze. Whatever fight he's forced into his words doesn't show in his expression in the least. I take him in slowly, calculating what's going on with him. His intentions, his motives.

"I want to see Laura and I want to get both of us out of here," I say, making my demand.

"I wanted you in here for something other than attempted bank robbery. For the murder of the men who broke into Laura's place." He's casual as he talks, slowly leaning back in his seat.

"Is that why you're keeping me in here? To get me to confess?" I practically hiss the words, low and full of venom.

"You won't. No man who'd let a woman take the fall—"

"I didn't let her do anything!" My fists land on the table, halting him in his place. The pressure of my jaw slamming shut to keep the thoughts at bay is too much. I swear I hear my teeth crack.

She never should have left me that night. If she'd stayed with me and never gone back to her apartment, none of this would have happened.

I never should have told her.

That's where we went wrong. I told her the ugly truth and she left. She always wanted to leave. Laura's not the kind of girl who stays, but damn I need her to. I need her back.

Everything slips back into place; my mask, my self-control. All I have to do is get her back. There's no more bad shit she doesn't know about. We'll be fine. I'll help her. I'll be her prince who saves her from this hell and she'll love me again. She can forgive me. She has to. Either that, or I'll lie. I say I don't know what she's talking about. I'll tell her I must've been drunk off my ass to come up with a lie like that. I'll do whatever I have to in order to get her back. What's done is done, but now we move forward. There's no other choice. It's a slow ease that overcomes my body. I flex my hand before looking back into Walsh's gaze. It's going to be all right. I can keep this from happening again. This is the worst of it. I know it is. It can't get worse than this.

"I'd like her out of here," I add, staring him in the eyes, "since we both know she didn't do anything wrong."

"She's being charged with murder."

"Is that what you told them?" I can't keep the anger down. "You're really going to hurt her to get to me?"

His eyes are piercing, his expression merciless. "I don't want either of you in here," he barely speaks. It's nearly impossible for me to hear and his lips don't move. I almost think I imagined it.

The next time he speaks, it's clear and spoken with intention. "You want to see her?"

The lack of trust separates us. It'll never be there. Ever.

"You should really see her," Cody adds when I don't answer. The air in the room changes. It's colder, deadlier.

"Then take me to her," I demand, but my power is limited on this side of the interrogation room.

"I have people to talk to," he says and rises from his seat as I curse under my breath, hating him and hating all of this. The scratch of metal is searing. A beep precedes the door opening and with his back to me once again he tells me, "This isn't how I thought things were going to happen."

Chapter 9

Laura

Walters shut up real quick the second Bernard came back to the cell. I don't know anything more than I wasn't supposed to kill Jean. He didn't give me that shiv to kill her and that knowledge makes me sick. But what other option did I have?

With no one here and my imagination running away with itself, I feel like I'm drowning.

If Marcus put out a hit on me, I'm dead. Maybe I got Jean first, but she gave me the upper hand by telling me. Sitting here all alone and not knowing a damn thing... I'm nothing but haunted and scared.

This room is larger. Bigger and without a mirror. It still seems like an interrogation room though even if I don't see any cameras at all. Wrapping my arms around myself, I sit back down in the lone chair, glancing at the small bed on the other side. It's not like a holding cell, because there's a solid door with a small window at eye height.

I don't know what this room is, but the bed, the lack of cameras, the unknown... it's fucking terrifying. All I can do is glance from the bed, back to the door, praying whoever comes through it will tell me something, *anything*, about what's going on.

I just want to get out of here. I can't take it. I don't like who I've become in here.

How long did it take for me to lose it? To lose the morality Nurse Roth has every day at work.

I search the walls for an answer to my rhetorical question and then belatedly remember there's not even a clock in here. Nothing at all to indicate the time. A humorless huff leaves me, and I close my eyes with it. Sleep is so tempting, and the bed is so close.

I can't sleep without knowing. There's a vent on the other side of the room that clicks on and off, keeping the room temperate. It's gone off six times now. That's the only way I've managed to keep track of time.

With my arms wrapped around my shoulders, I rock gently, trying to calm myself down. I haven't gotten my medicine yet. The set of four pills I have to take daily. I have faith, albeit a small bit of faith, that they'll provide them once another twenty-four hours have gone by. I can track time that way. I haven't slept, so I don't know how close I am to that time frame. Four pills once in the morning. I should be getting them soon, shouldn't I?

A shudder runs through my body, followed by a wave of nervous heat. With my eyes closed but my head leaning back, I keep rocking and pray that this will end. *Please let this be the worst of it.*

My eyes are too itchy, too worn out to cry anymore. I'm at the lowest low I could possibly be. *Please make it stop.* When I lick my dry lips, tasting the residue of salt from former tears, a loud beep warns me that God may have heard my prayers.

Does he find me worthy though? I don't dare to truly consider the question, because I'm certain the answer is quite firmly no.

A deep inhale doesn't settle my racing pulse as the heavy door, this one metal and most likely once a shiny silver, but now worn to a dull gray, opens with a heave and a groan.

"I'll tell you when," a voice says softly. The door stays open and a mumbled conversation is blocked by it, as is my view of the person belonging to that voice.

Seth. *Please, God*, I think and my lip quivers with a raw mix of hope and fear. I know it's his voice.

I'm not in control of my body when the door finally shuts with a resounding click and he becomes my sole focus. My heart cracks and splinters at the sight of him. The space between us vanishes and it's all my doing. He's frozen where he is, not moving, not reacting, simply watching me.

"Oh my God," I say and I can't help how both my expression and voice crumple. With a shaky hand over my mouth and the other on his jaw, I ask, "What happened?"

My gaze roams over his face. His stubble is so long it's scratchy and I've never seen such dark circles resting beneath his eyes before. "Have you even slept?" I ask before he can answer. My thumb brushes along a bruise as I murmur, "What did you do?" I can't stop touching him or asking him questions without even granting him a moment to answer.

There's a cut on his lip and I touch that too, gently, but I imagine it still stings. I have to hold my own hand, snatching it in my other and taking a step back. He looks like he's been thrown over the edge of a rocky cliff and managed to survive but hasn't slept in weeks.

I don't bother asking about the gunshot. Gripping the edge of his shirt, I pull it up, taking in the stitches and feeling a slight sense of respite at the sight.

He's alive. He's been taken care of, but... "What happened?"

I'm stricken, taking in every inch of him and not knowing a damn thing.

His warmth envelops me first. It's everywhere at once. Every inch of my skin is affected by his embrace. I don't move, afraid he'll move in response. It feels so good to be held. It feels like heaven to be safe in his arms. I bury my head in his chest when he shushes me. Shushes me! But still, his voice is the most comforting thing I've had in what feels like years.

My mind rewinds the days, stopping at the moment I saw him drunk and disgraced in his house. I have to close my eyes tight, ignoring the reminder of where that led. I can't. I can't not be held by him right now.

I know somewhere inside of me I hate him. I hate what he's done. The fact that he helped me mourn... At the thought I have to wipe my eyes and as I raise my arm, Seth creeps backward, but I'm quick to fist his shirt in my hand and shove my body against his. It's not a conscious move, it's like everything else that I've done since I've set foot in this place: it's an act to survive.

I know I hate him or at least what he did, but I need him. I selfishly need him right now. Is it possible to love someone, or at least crave to be loved by them while also hating them?

Simultaneously? I don't know that it is because it's only one way for me. Like the teeter-totter of a child's seesaw, I go from one to the other. Back and forth. But never both at once.

As my breath shakes and my shoulders press into his hard chest, I only love him right now. It kills me to see him hurt, and the idea of leaving this room without him destroys me.

At the thought, my eyes widen and I pull my head back so I can look him in the eyes. My hot face feels the instant chill of the air as I search his blue gaze for some sign of what's happening.

He still doesn't speak.

"Please, say something."

"The guard just told me something," he says and his voice is raw and pained.

Shattered is what I feel. There is zero doubt that any other word could describe it better. Broken and in disarray, all I can do is wait. His throat tightens when he swallows, his eyes holding nothing but regret in them. I'm fucked. That's all I can think. They have good evidence on the murder in my apartment or hell, the murder in my cell. Fuck! Fuck! How did this happen? I just want to scream.

My gaze falls as he tells me, "They told me..." he trails off and doesn't finish.

My hand is still wrapped around his shirt.

Something awful, something dreadful. If I could will myself to release him and back away, I would. But I can't. I physically can't. I'd rather be stuck here, a shattered girl unable to hate a man who's hurt me more than he'll ever know because I desperately need him to love me right now... yet all he bears for me is more bad news. Something to drag me farther into this hell.

"They told me you that you killed someone. I'm so fucking sorry, Laura. I don't know how you could ever forgive me."

My eyes rise slowly to meet his.

Thump, my heart skitters as Seth attempts to keep his expression schooled, not letting the sorrow take over although it's so close to doing just that already.

It takes me a long moment to realize he's apologizing and that this is about Walters and Jean.

"It's about Jean?" I question him, finding a bit of hope. It loosens my grip on him and I'm damn quick to tighten it the moment I'm aware of it. "That look in your eyes and what the guards told you? They know? Who knows? What did they say?" The series of breakneck questions is nothing at all like the initial ones. I rise up, not letting go of him and pulling myself closer to him as his expression morphs to something else entirely.

"Only the men who need to know, know. Everyone else is convinced its suicide. Or they better be, for their own good. Are you okay?"

He searches my expression, probably finding a hint of relief.

"I'm fine. And what about you?" I say and swallow, trying to calm myself. His hand covers my fisted one and I watch as his thumb grazes my skin. "What happened to you?" I whisper.

"Not here," he answers in a single breath then looks behind him at the window of the heavy metal door. "Soon though," he tells me and pulls my hand from his shirt, lifting my knuckles to his lips and kissing them.

The revolving door of emotions is endless.

"What else did they tell you?" I find myself crossing my arms over my chest, closer to my heart. If he has eyes and ears in this place, does he know... I try to swallow but it hurts.

With everything that's happened, I forgot for a small moment. I forgot about my heart giving up on me.

I watch every detail of Seth's face. I see the confusion in the twitch of his brow. "Are you okay? What else happened?" he bites out, coming closer to me and glancing at the window. "Did anyone do anything at all to you?" The way he asks the question, with the pain so evident, I'll never be able to look at him and hate him.

This man would do anything for me. I know he would. I've always known that though.

"No," I say and ease his worry. "No one did anything."

"I never should have..." Seth trails off and shakes his head, then wraps his arms around my waist. He pulls me in closer and I let him. I need it more than anything.

"You forgive me?" he questions, and his gaze pierces through me. Intense, raw, needy.

"Yes," I answer and I don't even know what for.

"Good," he says then breathes in deeply, still holding my hand to his lips and the warm breath sends a shudder to run down my arm and over my shoulder. He kisses each knuckle again and although I have question after question, I'm quietly waiting for more.

I get nothing, but at the same time, it's everything. He holds me for the longest time and it's the safest I've felt in God knows how long. Until he speaks.

"None of this should have happened," he tells me and I

hear him swallow, my cheek pressed against his chest. "You and I will work. We will be okay, but I need to punish you for running."

My arm yanks back in an attempt to rip my hand away, but Seth's grip is unyielding. So firm it nearly hurts. Seething, I aim to bite back some response that involves the phrase *fuck you* or maybe *you're out of your damn mind*, but the heat and intensity coming off of Seth in waves silences me.

He means it. He's dead set on whatever it is he's concocted in his head. My heart flips and pauses like it does when he's around. As if the medicine has run its course and I need another dose.

The whirlwind of what my life is pauses when I look back into Seth's gaze.

Did they tell him about my heart? I find myself staring at the small tinted window as if it has answers for me. *Did they tell him everything? Or just about Jean?*

He would have said something. He would have. I know he would have brought it up if he knew.

He goes on about how I run. I can barely focus on his words, because all I can think about is my heart and how Seth will react when he finds out.

I can only stare into his beautiful eyes, listening to his voice, knowing he's here in front of me, here to keep me safe. I don't think they told him. I don't think he knows. I don't want him to. I'd rather he not have that to weigh him down like it does me. I hate this, the uncertainty. The pressure. Everything is falling to pieces but I need to be strong for the time I have left.

"Babygirl, you're mine. You know that, don't you?"

I'm nodding my head before I'm even aware of it.

"We're going to be fine, but you need to have your ass blistered red for running."

How can he bring it up so easily? I ran because of what he confessed and here he is, talking about it in this way. As if all of this is my fault. My heart ticks erratically again and I find it hard to care about it. I need him. I need Seth to hold me right now.

"Don't cry." Seth's voice is gentle but firm. He takes a half step closer to me so there's no space between us. "I can't let this happen again," he tells me.

I didn't even know I was crying. I hate how easily I cry now. Am I broken entirely? This is what it's like to be ruined.

"It won't happen again," I tell him in a whisper.

Finally releasing my hand, he wraps both of his arms around me and I let myself fall forward. *None of it matters.* He rocks me and I pretend not to feel the weight of my reality.

"I won't let anything happen to you," Seth promises me, kissing my hair. "You'll be out of here soon and then you'll stay with me. You're not allowed to leave me again."

His voice is what brings back tears to my eyes. These fucking tears. All I've done is cry. I should be through with them by now. But he's so sure, so certain of himself that I'll never leave him again. I can hear it in his tone and how much determination and hope are present there. If only he keeps me by his side, everything will be fine. As if he's capable of that. He doesn't know my heart is withered and frail. He doesn't know it can't last.

I wish I'd never loved him, so he'd never know the loss.

My hot tears soak into his shirt and I ignore them. He hushes me and rocks me, and finally he bends down to kiss me.

His kiss is everything I need; comforting but demanding, strong and yet loving. I pour everything I have into it, deepening it, parting my lips and feeling my body mold to his.

A deep, rough groan rumbles his chest and that only makes me crave more. More of him while I can have it. More of this while I'm able.

But Seth denies me, grabbing my small hands in his and lifting his head to breathe with his eyes closed.

"I have to punish you. Whether you hate me or not." I can't answer and the silence forces him to look at me. "You can hate me while I punish you, but you're not leaving me. Ever."

Ever.

A younger version of me, an unknowing one, would fall in love with that word. We don't get to decide how long our forever lasts, though. It's naïve to think we can.

"Seth, I'm not okay," I whisper and wish I could take it back. He can't know. I don't know why I said it.

A small bit of relief overcomes me when he answers, "I know."

"I'm losing myself," I say and grant him a small truth and rewind again. Rewind to a moment I felt the distance between who I thought I was and who I really am.

"I know," he repeats with nothing but sympathy.

"I... killed someone." I whisper the rugged confession as if he's not already aware.

"But you're here, with me. I won't let them take you away." I'm torn and twisted.

"They're going to come for me and they're going—"

"To either put you back in a cell with me, or to release us both. I made sure of it."

Chapter 10

Seth

She's always looked this beautiful but the thought of losing her makes her skin look softer, more delicate. She's fragile beneath me.

Breathing in deep, the smell of her hair lingers in my lungs. She's okay. She's here in my arms. She's letting me hold her. I have to remind myself of the three bits of my reality. They're the only things that matter right now. Her skin touching mine, her trusting me, relying on me.

Thank fuck. I can fix this. I can make it all better.

I can't believe she killed that woman, though. Shock doesn't describe my reaction at all when I was informed.

I fucking hate myself for not being there. Walters said they didn't want to let on that they knew about the hit on Laura and they knew that Jean was in there to kill her. Whoever hired Jean Cinders would have known if they'd switched Laura's cell. So instead Jase and Carter waited for the note that was supposed to be coming. The men I trusted most gave that order. To wait and watch.

She isn't bait, though. My girl isn't bait and he should've known better than to let her sit there with that hitman. I might hate myself but I hate Jase and Carter too. They risked her life by allowing her to stay in that cell. They knew she was there and in danger, and they just let her sit there. How could they do that? If it'd been Bethany or Aria, that woman never would have been in that cell. Not for a second.

Walters said they were told to wait, to sit on it and wait for the next move.

In the meantime, Jase wanted to show Laura that she was protected and safe. But by giving her a fucking weapon? None of these people know Laura. She doesn't trust easily and when she's scared, she'll do anything to survive. He's a fucking idiot and I'll never trust him again with her. Never.

Kissing her temple, I smooth down her hair. She's sweet and loving, but my God if you try to hurt her, she'll hurt you first swift and severe. I should be grateful though, because she hasn't turned that venom on me yet. Even though I deserve it.

"Everything will be fine," I promise her and I mean every bit of it. "I'll make damn sure of it."

"I love you," she tells me and presses her forehead into my chest when she starts to cry again, turning her head down as if I won't be able to see. God, to hear her tell me that again. I'm not worthy. I kiss her hair again and again, wanting to say it back but refusing to give her those words for the first time in this room.

She has to know I love her more than anything. And I'll tell her just that, the moment we're back home where we belong.

Clinging to me, she rocks her body and I can feel how heavy she becomes as sleep attempts to pull her under.

I glance at the room for the first time. It's meant for conjugal visits. She shouldn't have to be in this position at all, let alone here. Looking at the bed, I hate myself for fucking up so badly that she's in this room at all.

"I hate these clothes on you." The subconscious thought leaves me before I realize I've spoken the words aloud.

"Orange isn't my color." She whispers the small joke back to me. Sleep drenches it but the hint of the girl I knew long ago is still there.

I can't close my eyes without seeing her alone in a cell, ready to kill in order to survive. Even as I stare at the back wall, the cinder blocks play the scene for me as I imagine how it went down. I know hate and I know love.

I hate myself but I love her.

It's as simple as that.

"You should lie down and sleep," I say, deciding not to

tell her we may be here, in this room, until tomorrow. I don't know how long it'll take for my men to do my bidding and push the issue of keeping Laura in here when she has a solid self-defense argument. No judge should have allowed it and the lawyers are working on having it overruled. My one call went to Jase and he filled me in. It could be hours to have the initial ruling overturned. Or it could be days, depending on how easily the judge can be convinced. He isn't one we have in our back pocket.

"Come with me." With her lips grazing my shirt, Laura peers up at me, begging me, "Please."

It doesn't escape my notice that she hasn't let go of me since I've walked in here. She tried once at the thought of being punished for running away.

I should tell her what it does to me to have her want me like she does. Just as I should carry out the punishment. If I'm harder with her, more stern, she'll be safe. She'll see; it'll be for the good of us both. It's what we need.

"We just need to get out of here," I speak without thinking, a tired sigh escaping with it. With my hand tangled in her hair, I kiss her forehead at the same time that she kisses the dip in my throat.

A spike of want runs rampant inside of me. I don't know what I anticipated from her, probably another punch to the face, but I sure as hell didn't expect her affection.

"Please come lie down with me," she begs again in a whisper

and with her doe eyes looking up at me, I can't say no.

"All right." Giving in, I walk her hand in hand to the small bed. The bed creaks and shifts as I lie down, keeping my upper half propped up and my eyes on the door. She crawls in just how she used to, and lays her head on my chest, searching for a comfortable position. Years of this and she always settles on my bicep, but starts on my chest.

"This takes me back," I comment.

"What?" she questions sleepily and looks at me through her thick lashes. I have to smile down at her, even if it is a sad one because comparing what we had before to what we have now only makes me feel regret.

"Nothing, just this bed is so small... like the one at your grandmother's house."

Her wide eyes go soft blue for a moment, and she gives me the same smile in return before she sinks back down. The kind of smile that doesn't reach your eyes. I take my time pulling the blanket around her, tucking her in and then settle back against the wall.

"Sleep." I give her the command when her small fingers trace every little cut on my hand rather than being still.

"Did they tell you what happened in the holding cell?"

"Your panic attack?"

She stares up at me, her lips parted slightly like a word is caught there. "Were you faking it?" I tease her, downplaying it so she doesn't freak out. I can't blame her. Out of all the things to be, she shouldn't be embarrassed about it, and that's a bit how she looks. I nudge my shoulder, forcing her to roll toward me and her small hand splays against my chest to catch herself. "I was going to tell the guys there's no way you were faking it, you've never been good at faking it."

My crude joke gets the smallest hint of a laugh from her. It's short but it brings a genuine smile to her lips. "You'll be all right," I promise her. "We'll get out of here and I'll keep you safe."

She doesn't protest what I say and I pray that it means she's let go of what I told her about her father. At least for the moment. I'll tell her everything if she wants. If she wants to ignore it, forget it, deny it, I'll let that happen too. Whatever I have to do to keep her.

It takes me a long moment as I'm staring at the knob of the door, trying not to replay that scene from all those years ago, to realize she's crying.

"So many tears," I tease her gently, but lean down to wipe the tears from her left eye. The tears from her right are stolen by my shirt.

"I just want to be safe with you," she whispers and then sniffs. She always looks pissed off rather than hurt when she cries. She doesn't now, though.

"You are safe with me," I say and I can't hide the despair in my tone at the thought that she doesn't feel safe with me. "You want to go when we get out of here?" I search for anything, grasping for a thread to hold on to and all I can think is that she never wanted this life. If I'd left eight years ago, given it all up, none of this would have happened. "We can go wherever you want. We can leave. As long as we're together."

Her sobs turn harder and she crawls onto my lap, no longer satisfied with only having her cheek on my chest. Her small form curls up as she rests her head in the crook of my neck. Wrapping both of my arms around her, I hold her tighter, not remembering a time she's been like this. She's so broken. My poor girl.

"I'm sorry," I whisper into her hair, stroking her back, doing everything I can to love her. "We're going to be fine." My throat is tight with emotion when I promise her, "If you want to get out of here and leave, I promise I'll leave. I'll do it for you."

She doesn't respond, other than to cry harder. I shush her, I kiss her, I don't know what else to do. I wish I'd just left with her eight years ago. I wish we had a different life together.

"Let it out, Babygirl." Still rocking her, I watch the door and let her fall apart. I'll be here for her always. She'll see. I mean it and when she sees that, she'll stay with me. I just can't lose her again.

She doesn't respond to the idea of us leaving and part of me thinks it's because she doubts I'll do it. "I'll do anything to keep you," I whisper when her sobs quiet.

She doesn't respond to that either. She sits up all on her

own, her ass still in my lap and avoids eye contact. It's not uncommon for her to do that after a cry. With her nose red and her cheeks only slightly less so, she picks up the sheet and wipes her eyes.

"I'm sorry." That's the first thing she says.

"Nothing to be sorry about," I say, pressing my hand to her cheek and she leans into my touch. It's the first bit of hope I have when she closes her eyes and puts both her hands over mine. Her bottom lip trembles again and she asks, "Can I ask you, please, to hold me until the end?"

"To the very end," I promise her and she tries her damnedest not to cry again. Her eyes stay closed and I have to pull her in close because she sits there, not moving, not saying anything. "I promise you, it's going to be all right. Better than. I promise, I'll fix it all."

Time passes, a lot of it, before she tells me, "I know you will." It's only a gentle whisper until sleep takes her away from me.

I can't breathe. I know I'm able to, but I can't breathe. Clinging to Seth, I can't do anything but hold him closer and try to get rid of the vision in front of my eyes. It was a nightmare but then I woke up here. It really happened.

I killed her.

My eyes burn and I heave in a breath.

"Laura, it's okay. It's okay." Seth's trying to soothe me. He's doing everything he can, but the nightmare felt so real. I woke up only to remember it happened. It happened.

Slowly, I can move, although I'm trembling. "I need it to go away," I speak into his chest. Seth smells like home. He doesn't smell like here. If only I'd been sleeping closer...

I inch myself onto his lap. I don't want to touch any of the bed, only him.

Make it go away. Erase all of it. I want it all gone.

"Hey, hey, you okay?" he says. His voice is a balm, but his touch is salvation.

"Just hold me," I beg him, finally coming down from the terror. With his arms wrapped around me as I'm cradled in his lap, I lift up my head and tell him, "No, no, just kiss me."

Crashing my lips to him, I refuse to feel anything but him. He'll take me away from here. He'll save me. I know he will. His lips are hot, my kiss hungry.

At first he tries to pull back, although his lips have already softened and molded to mine, teasing me.

"Laura—" he starts, in almost a warning tone.

"Please," I say, cutting him off. "Please, Seth. Please kiss me." I am as desperate and pathetic as I sound. I'm so very aware of it.

The room isn't dark or small but either way, it feels like it's closing in on me. "I need you," I breathe with my eyes closed.

He can take me away from here. He can make me feel like it's all going to be all right. He's done it so many times before.

All of my darkest moments are only blips, only small dips in a timeline because he was there showing me where to go, leading me away. He can do it all with a kiss.

"Kiss me," I tell him, although it comes out as if I'm begging. "I'll do anything for you to kiss me right now." I'm slow to open my eyes, my heart steady as my hands move up to his neck. His muscles ripple under my touch as he leans in with me, nipping my bottom lip then sucking it before finally kissing me.

Gratitude swarms with desire, the two swirling deep in my belly. His smell, his touch, his kiss. I want it all surrounding me, protecting me and making it all go away.

Neither of us breathe as we kiss and in the moment of passion, we break away, gasping for air as his hands roam down my body. "Please," I beg him.

My legs part for him, straddling him already although we're both clothed. "Laura." My name is both a warning and the only word Seth speaks.

I say please, with longing.

He says Laura, with a torturous tone.

As he lays me on my back, I keep his lips to mine, parting my own and licking along the seam of his until he parts them, deepening the kiss and melding our mouths together.

The feel of his length pressing against my leg is all I need to moan. He doesn't make a move to undress either of us, so I do it. Ignoring his protests and stroking him before he can tell me not to.

I open my eyes to see his head arched back, his deep groan of pleasure filling the space. He towers over me with all this power, and with a single touch, I know he wants me. I know he'll do everything he can to make sure I feel the same way I make him feel.

A faint beat flickers in my chest and I love it. I love that he makes me feel all of this. "I want you," I beg him as my hand moves to his velvety head.

I already know I'm ready for him when his heated gaze drops to meet mine. Both of our lips are parted, our breathing heavy. Both of us in need.

I shimmy out of my pants, dropping them to the side of the small bed, all the while keeping my eyes on Seth. He doesn't move, his hands fisted and digging into the mattress on either side of my head. His shirt still on, but his pants are pushed down to his knees.

If someone were to walk in on us in this moment, they'd get a sight of his fine ass. And the very thought of it makes me smile. It's a small smile, but it shows.

I think that's what does it, that and the last *please* I have to give him, for Seth to lower his body down to mine.

He props up one of my legs with the crook of his arm, spreading and angling me. His lips drop to mine at the same time that he enters me. The motion is swift and harsh. The act tears a scream from my throat, but he catches it. Staying deep inside of me, Seth whispers, "You will be quiet."

It's a statement that makes my heart pound with desire.

"I will." The whisper is lost in his kiss as he moves at a slower pace, each stroke deep before pulling out nearly all the way. Every time he moves backward, I pray for him to come back. Each thrust forward is nearly too much though, stinging my eyes with tears as my nails dig into his back and my head thrashes.

It's torturously sweet and slow. My pleasure builds, taking its time and feeling like the highest of highs before crashing down. I can't kiss him when I do. Tears leak from my eyes while the convulsion of the strongest orgasm I've ever had paralyzes my body and I bite down on his shoulder to keep from screaming out.

SETH

The knock at the door is followed by it opening, only a couple of inches. Laura is sound asleep on my shoulder and even though my arm is fucking numb, I haven't moved.

Carefully, I maneuver my way out from under her, hating

that I have to leave her at all. I'm afraid if I leave, she'll remember why she left. Not that she can go anywhere in here, but she could realize she doesn't want me. I can't let that happen. All of this is too good to be true and I'm waiting for the other shoe to drop.

Staring down at her, I make sure she's asleep. Her readjusting and inhaling deeply is followed by the smallest of hums and not a stir afterward.

On the short walk to the door I shake out my arm, trying to bring it back to life. I'm tired as all hell. My eyes feel it, my body feels it, and all I want is to fall asleep with Laura in my own bed.

When I pull open the door wider, I catch sight of Walters first and I'm concerned by the expression he gives me until he nods his head behind him, at fucking Cody Walsh.

My gaze moves back to Walters. Walsh isn't on our payroll and whatever truce that was between us is long gone as far I'm concerned. My jaw hardens, and I play out every way this can go in my mind.

Before I can say a word, Walsh speaks up. "We're letting you both go."

His eyes don't look past me but even still, I shut the door to hide the sight of Laura sleeping from him and speak quietly. "Is that right?"

"The DA came to the decision. We don't have enough to charge either of you."

"And the cases?" I ask Walsh but look back at Walters, nodding and dismissing him.

"Yours is closed. Hers is still open."

I don't respond, pissed off and knowing that I need the Cross brothers to cover my ass in that case. I hate them for leaving her in that cell. It needs to go away in an instant, though, and they have far more pull than I do. I haven't forgotten that I promised her I'd leave, and I will. The second she says the word, we'll go wherever she wants. I don't know what that means for me and Jase. I know I'll lose her again if I don't, though. I'm willing to do anything. Anything and everything.

Walsh speaks when I don't say anything. "Passing out at the wheel is your defense, in case you didn't know." The humor isn't lost on me, but I don't show a hint of it to him.

I can't stand the sight of Walsh after he kept me in that room for as long as he did. I could have been with Laura sooner; I could have stopped the bullshit that was going on behind the scenes in her cell if he hadn't kept me in that damn interrogation room.

As far as I'm concerned, Walsh can go fuck himself.

"And self-defense against a dirty cop is hers."

I know the lawyer will tell me what he's talking about, but lawyers only know so much. "Care to elaborate?" I ask, needing to know the intel on the cop involved in her case.

"He had no reason to be there, or to be with the other men.

He was undercover, but not on a case that involved them."

I nod, peeking back at Laura for only a moment and ensuring she's still passed out.

"Thank you." He earns a single point of gratitude for giving me that information. He can still go fuck himself, though.

"I wasn't going to let her go down for your mistake." Walsh's voice is harsh and my grip on the doorframe turns white knuckled. "I didn't know how close you two were until last week. I looked up everything between you two, and I think I have a good idea of what went down."

The guilt is there and I know he's right, but I don't like him. I'll never like him.

He must know exactly what I'm thinking from my glare because he tells me, "We don't have to be on the same side, but you don't know the shit I had to pull to get you both out of here."

Jase said it could take days to get to the judge and this is faster than I thought it'd be, but I doubt Walsh's honesty.

"That judge would have never turned. Judge Lainson wants the Cross brothers and he knows you and her are a way to get in."

"So you convinced him that the cases were too weak to hold up in court?" I ask, still not believing what he's telling me. He could simply be taking the credit.

"No, I didn't. I had the DA get involved and told him about an incident with Lainson. All of his cases have been handed over."

"An incident?"

"It doesn't involve you. What matters is that your case was given to a different judge because of it. A judge who happens to be on your payroll."

I'm silent, searching his gaze for honesty and that's exactly what I find.

Walsh looks over his shoulder, down the deserted hall and a look of shame is barely registered on his face. "I did what I had to do. You don't have to like me; I don't have to like you either. But I'm very aware that you and the brothers are the fastest way for me to get what I want." He looks past me, not able to see much at all in the room and then meets my gaze. "Get her, and get out. I'll get Walters for you since you seem to have a preference."

He doesn't fail to remind me, "Remember this, King. You owe me."

I only nod in agreement. That I do. For the first time since I met this asshole, I'm grateful for him.

"As a show of good faith," he says and looks as if he's debating something but decides to say it, "the evidence I have on you and Jase, it's in the mail."

"You have backups." It's not a question. Any smart man would.

"Had," he corrects. "I don't think you realize what he did to me. All I want is Marcus. None of this matters and

I'm willing to risk a lot to ensure Marcus and I meet sooner, rather than later."

"Why do you want Marcus so much?" I have to ask. He's gone out of his way to help me... all for Marcus?

His lips set in a straight line and he stares at me for a moment. "A while ago, he let things happen to a woman I cared about. He knew she was at risk, and he allowed them anyway." The last bit morphs into a harshly spoken whisper. He nods, staring at the crack in the door rather than at me. "She forgave him because he saved her from the end. But he was never held accountable. He believes every action has a consequence. He needs to have his. She forgave him, but I didn't."

Chapter 11

Laura

"You're on the DA's watch list. Stay here. Stay low. That's my professional advice." The lawyer is a no-nonsense man. In a sharp suit and with even sharper deep brown eyes, he's laid out everything for Seth and me.

"I understand." Seth's response is professional even though he's dressed in plaid flannel pants and a white t-shirt, both of which he slept in, and his lower right jaw is still bruised. The two of them are at complete odds in appearance, but one hundred percent in agreement on what happened.

I was meant to be leverage to get an in for the judge to take down the Cross brothers. They didn't care about the cop. This wasn't the first time the cop cut through red tape and was caught doing things he shouldn't have been. They knew. They withheld information in order to charge me.

My mind has wandered most of the meeting. It's late and I'm still tired. I don't think I slept for very long in that room with Seth. I've never been one to be happily woken up from sleep but hearing Seth tell me softly that we could leave? My eyes jolted open at that and I got my ass moving, still half asleep, just to get out of there.

"Always a pleasure," Seth says and the two men stand, the lawyer giving a polite laugh to the joke. They're shaking hands by the time I stand up and I reach out my own. Mr. Grayson's hair is swept back on the top and short on the sides. He has a look to him that's nothing but clean cut. He even apologized to me when he used profanity.

I don't know how he got involved with the Cross brothers and Seth, but I'm grateful for him and his insight. There's no way the case will stay open. He's sure of it.

Seth's arm wraps around my lower back as he walks the lawyer to the door, smiling while the lawyer insists that I'll be fine now that the investigation regarding the cop truly has no legs to stand on. It seems easy enough, case closed, but from the look in Seth's eye, the way the smile on his face is only polite like the lawyer's laugh, he's hiding something. And the second the door closes, I turn in his embrace, take a step back and question him.

"Why is he saying it's over and done, yet you're acting like it's not?"

Seth's jaw is lined with a rough coat of stubble. It's dark and combined with the bruise, his charming look is gone. He's rough and deadly but even still, the smirk he gives me and the gentle peck he places on my lips make him nothing but the man I remember him to be.

I'm a hair's breadth away from laying into him for not answering me, but he does. Honestly, and it makes a part of me wish he had lied. "Because it's not over."

"Legally—"

"Legally, we have nothing to worry about," he agrees with me, cutting me off and using his other arm to pull me into him. As if this one will be more effective than the last. And truthfully, I don't want to fight him. I don't want to leave his hold so long as he's giving me what I need. Right now, that's information.

"The guy I killed wasn't only a crooked cop. I think he-and the rest of them—worked for Marcus and I think whatever they started, isn't over."

"The mention of that name..." I trail off as chills flow from the base of my skull down my spine. The name elicits fear because it comes from years of whispers and authority.

"He's only a man."

"Why though? Why would Marcus want anything to do with me?" It doesn't take more than a second of staring up at Seth to know that he's the reason why. I am only a pawn. "What did you do?"

"I'm not sure it's him. When I know, I'll tell you."

It's silent as we move out of the foyer but then I remember something.

"Delilah wrote a lot of things in her books; some were about cops. She was a lawyer, you know. She knew things." I wish I were rested and had a better memory. I can't for the life of me recall a single name or anything specific about the men Marcus 'worked with.' "Maybe something useful is in her notebooks."

"Declan's looking," is all Seth responds but it's enough to ease my worry... some.

"You really think it was Marcus?" I question him. There was never a time in my life where I thought, *I'm going to be on the end of that man's wrath.* I never even wanted to see him. I wanted to pretend he was only a myth. Seth is right though; Marcus is only a man.

He's one I'm terrified of, though. And now he has men working for him. Which is the first I've ever heard of this.

"I don't know," Seth answers me grimly, taking his time to sit on the couch and instead of retaking my seat on the chair where I was during the briefing, I settle down next to him. I can't explain it, but right now I have to be touching Seth.

It feels too lonely, too cold when he's not right there. Not only that, but I'm still scared. I know I don't have to be. I'm safe here, but it's easier to not be scared when someone's holding your hand.

Just as Seth is holding mine now. He lifts my hand in his and stares at it when he talks. "I'm going to lay low but do some digging. I want you to stay here."

"I have work."

"I know, and you'll be safe there. Jase is sending some guys to watch the place."

I peek up past the living room windows and note the lights from a quarter mile outside on the edge of Seth's property. "Like he has guys watching out there."

"Yeah, they're on watch right now. Everything is safe and protected as long as you're here, at the Cross estate or at work." His steely blues hit me hard when he tells me, "If you go anywhere else, tell me. They'll follow you and keep you safe. That way I can work, knowing you're all right." He's looking at me with his brow raised as if I wouldn't tell him.

"I don't have a death wish," I try to joke but the mention of death forces me to subconsciously raise my hand to my chest. It splays over my heart and I consider for only a half second telling Seth about my condition and then I do what I've been doing. I drop it and my hand, using my other to squeeze his hand tighter.

The plan right now regarding my systolic heart failure diagnosis: I'm going to call and make an appointment with the specialist and until that appointment, I'm going to take my medicine and pretend like pills will fix it. I would rather hide it until I know what my options are.

"Hey." Seth's firm voice brings me back to problem A, away from problem... where does my heart even fall on the list? "Promise me you'll let me know where you are at every step and you'll listen."

A small submissive smile graces my lips, meant to appease him. "I promise, I'll listen."

With his hand still wrapped around mine, he taps my knuckles against his thigh rhythmically as he looks at me, searching for something. He doesn't like whatever he sees, judging by his expression, which is raw and open. He's undecided.

"What's wrong?" I question.

"It's just that I can see you taking off again, even though you're sitting there telling me that you won't. I know I want to prevent that and I know how, but you don't like the idea of being punished," he answers without hesitation. "See that?" He stops the rhythmic tapping and holds up our hands, still embraced but barely. "You tried to pull away at just the thought of it. And you did that yesterday too, when we were—"

"In jail," I finish the statement bitterly. I'm pissed that he has the nerve to bring it up again, but I don't want to fight. Swallowing, I press my fingers back between his and scoot closer to Seth. "I don't like the way you say it."

"Is that all? Because I don't think that's it. I don't think you want me to be..."

My gaze moves from his to the hole that's still in the wall.

I was able to clean up the pieces of drywall before the lawyer came in, but the remaining evidence of the other night is still there. I don't want it here. I don't want anything to do with it.

When I move to stand, I have to rip my hand away from Seth's. How dare he bring it up.

"You don't get to punish me for leaving because you told me you killed my father." I don't even know how I'm able to say the words. The truth kills me, it chokes me, it smothers me. I don't want it.

"That's not—"

"It is!" I scream at him, shaking my head wildly. I can't take it, and my heart races. I can't go through with this conversation. I simply can't control what it's doing to me. "Please don't do this. Don't hurt me like that."

"Is that what you think I want to do?" As he speaks, he raises his voice like I do. "I don't want to hurt you!" He says it like I've spoken something offensive. As if I'm in the wrong. A moment passes with silence and the next time he speaks, his voice is calmer, lower. His hands are in the air like he's approaching a wild animal. "It's not about hurting you."

"It's not about the act of punishing me," I say and it takes everything to get the words out. "It's why!" *Thump, thump, thump*, the beating races through me, and I struggle to breathe.

Calming myself, I try. I try to appease him while protecting myself. "My father wasn't a rat. You didn't kill him. I don't want to believe it."

"Laura, it's about you leaving—"

"Stop it. Both times. Both times I left..." My strength weakens and my pulse is hard in my veins. I'm hot all over. "Can't you understand? I don't want to remember why I left."

I cut him off the moment he tries to speak. "You can't bring it up. It brings it all back and I can't go back, Seth. I can't live in the past, not when my present—" My throat tightens, silencing the rest of my thought.

"I'm not trying to hurt you," he says. His tone is calming and I know he's telling the truth. I know he is, but I can't allow the mention of it. Everything tumbles downward after it. I can't stop the falling of memories.

"I'll make a truce," I offer him, desperate to end this. "I never bring it up, and you don't hold my sin over my head."

"What's that?" His question is softly spoken.

"I never left. I never left you. I had no choice. If you get to live with a lie, so do I."

Only feet apart, we couldn't be further away from one another. Both of us struggling, but we can live this way. I know we can. We can pretend and be happy. That's all I want right now, for a little while. All I have is a little while anyway.

"Can't we just pretend? Please," I beg him. "I don't want to remember why I left. You say you're going to punish me for it, but saying that only brings it all back up. I don't want that. I don't want to remember. Can't we just pretend?"

"We can't pretend that you don't leave when things get bad."

My voice raises and I slam my hand against his chest, trying to shove him away as my cadence cracks. "And you can't pretend that things aren't fucking horrific."

I can pretend all I want but we are so badly broken, and the realization weakens my knees. I'd fall if Seth wasn't still holding me.

"Please don't do this," I beg him again as he pulls me into his chest. "Please, I don't want to cry anymore."

Seth's hand on my shoulder, his forearm against my back, steadies me. He rocks me softly and it's completely at odds with everything else. We are so broken, but this is all I have and all I want. I've lived my life without Seth in it. I can't do that anymore despite everything I now know.

It's a whirlwind of emotions and betrayal, yet a constant in the storm is how he makes me feel when we're like this. Me, broken and not knowing how to fix myself and him, steadily holding me.

"I need you," I whisper. Pulling away from the warmth of his chest, I tell him, "I don't need you to punish me."

"I need to know you won't run." His answer is simple.

My gaze is beseeching. In an attempt to crack this armor he's put up, I say, "I'm telling you I won't."

His lips part and I can almost hear his unspoken words declaring that I told him that before. My heart stumbles and falls so quickly. "Seth, I can't leave you," I say and swallow thickly, needing to tell him that what little time I have left, I need to be with him. The truth doesn't come, though. What if he decides he can't be with me when I have a faulty heart? He can't love someone who's only going to leave him. After all, that's what I do. I leave him.

"I'm afraid," I admit, opting for a new truth. Barely breathing as my eyes turn glossy. Haphazardly wiping them, I hold on to the anger. I pull away from him to bitch, "I hate fucking crying. When did I—"

"You can cry." Seth's voice is calm when he takes my forearm, pulling me back into him.

I don't have enough time to cry.

"I'm afraid of this horrible side of me. It bothers me... how I always fall into this world. I'm drawn to it, Seth," I confess and look him in the eyes. "There's no point in leaving you when I know this bad piece of me is just who I am and it leads me into this... this..."

"Nothing about you is horri—"

I cut him off before he can console me and feed me some bullshit about how I don't have that in me. I know I do. It's there waiting and ready, almost greedily wanting to come out and prove itself. "There's plenty of bad in me! I killed a woman. I killed her. I—I—I—" Words fail me.

"You had to."

"A part of me *wanted* to," I confess.

"Calm down." With both of his hands on my shoulders,

he tells me sincerely, "There's nothing wrong with you."

"There is—" he doesn't let me finish.

"No there isn't."

He doesn't get it. He doesn't see the point.

"I can't leave you, Seth, because I accept it. I accept that I'll always be led back here. I promise you I won't leave. Because I know I need you." It's not all the truth, but it's jagged pieces of it. Reckless and scattered, but it's all true. "I won't ever leave you because I'm afraid of that side of me. But I know you understand it. I know you'll protect me from it all." That tiny last bit is so raw and honest that it shakes me to my core.

"Can I tell you something?" Seth asks and waits for me. I peek up at him, nodding.

A sad smile I know so well greets me. It's the kind he gives me when he tells me something he doesn't want to. "You're my good side."

My brow pinches with confusion until he leans in, kissing it, kissing that crease and then he says it again. "If there's a good side and a bad side to every person. You're my only good side. You can't leave me again. I'm nothing that I want to be without you. Imagine that feeling when that dark side threatens to take over. Imagine that, and only that."

Seth has been so steady, so strong, I haven't viewed him as broken, not like I view myself. Never. Not once.

All I can do, as quickly as my body is able, is to lean forward and hold on to him. No matter how hard I hug him, he hugs me closer, his warm breath in the crook of my neck. I wish I could just go back. There are times in life when I wished that, but never so much as now. Thinking back to that first time I saw him, I would change it all. I'd save us. We could have had a different life. I know in my heart he's the one I'm meant to be with, but why does this life have to end like this? Maybe in the next we'll remember. Maybe we'll remember this love and be drawn to one another again.

"I promise I won't ever leave your side. Just please, pretend with me. Please."

He doesn't say he'll pretend but when he kisses me, he promises not to bring it up again, and I'll take that.

"Can we just agree on one thing?" I dare to ask, to put it to bed and let it rest where it is. "I don't want you to bring up me leaving again. You don't want me to bring up," I have to pause and breathe in deep, pretending I'm not saying these words right now, "my father again."

Seth is still and quiet.

"Right?" I ask him, prodding him to agree with me.

"You have to know I'm sorry."

"Don't, Seth," I beg him, swallowing down the pain. "I need you to drop it, this talk about me leaving and needing to be punished for it. Drop it and never bring it up again and I'll do the same."

Seth doesn't say anything. He doesn't agree and he doesn't disagree. He holds me though, close and with a grip that isn't going to let up. That's all I want right now. With everything going on, this is all I need.

"Hey," I tell him, "I love you."

"That's all that matters," he answers and then kisses me. He's right. Right now, all that matters is this. I can be okay with this. I make sure I tell him, "I'll never stop loving you."

There's a moment when he's holding me, where I'm warm and so safe, that nothing else feels real. It simply can't be true because when we touch, everything is right. So all of the wrong that is happening around us, all of this awful shit, it's not real.

I let my lips slip up Seth's throat. There's always a little rough stubble there. The tip of my nose drags along it and when I inhale deeply, calming and settling, all I smell is him. I plant a small kiss right there, right on his throat and I'm awarded with a groan, deep and rough, vibrating against my entire front.

He readjusts and I know he must be hard for me. It's so easy to get him worked up, to get him wanting me. Truth be told, it's the same back. There isn't a moment where he kisses me and I don't want and need him instantly.

"You really love me still?" he questions with his piercing blue eyes focused solely on me. I'm so hurt inside. For him. For us.

"I could never not love you, Seth," I tell him honestly and kiss him before the swell of emotion takes over. All I want is him. To be held by him. To be loved by him. Everything else, in this moment, I choose to ignore.

Crashing my lips against his, I slip my hands up his shirt. One slides up while the other moves down, slipping past his waistband. I love the feel of him in my hand. How hard he is, yet soft and smooth. All of him was made to be a sex god. Every inch of his body. I grip him once and beg him, "Please," in a heated whisper.

Seth inhales and lets his head fall back. With his eyes still closed, he commands me, "Get your ass undressed now."

I can't help that I smile, that I feel a rush of warmth from my cheeks, down my chest, all the way down at the thought of him taking me right now. With my teeth digging into my bottom lip, I'm quick to remove every article of clothing. Seth is slower, lazily stripping as he watches me.

"I love it when you smile like that," he comments before pulling his shirt over his head.

"I love it when you make me smile like this," I tell him back, feeling a dull ache in my chest, a pull to him that I need to hold on to forever. Until my last breath. Because it's the best thing I have in this world. He's the only thing that feels good. This. This moment and what's between us, it's worth living for even if nothing else is.

Both of us bared, he stalks toward me and I wait, standing with anticipation, goosebumps traveling over my skin, but I'm so hot, the shiver doesn't come with an ounce of cold, only want.

He keeps his gaze pinned to mine until he has to break it to plant a single open-mouthed kiss in the crook of my neck. It's then that I reach out to him, both of my hands on his chest until I move them up to his shoulders. His hands roam my body and I squeal when he lifts me into his arms. His cock is nestled between my sex.

He braces my back against the wall and it doesn't escape my knowledge that the hole from the other night is still there, just to the right of me. That's where he fucks me, hard and ruthlessly.

He doesn't try to silence my strangled cries of pleasure. He tears them from me with each forceful thrust. His eyes never leave mine, even when he kisses my jaw.

"Seth," is the only word I can say as he takes me, pounding into me relentlessly. He hits the back of my wall every time and I swear it's too much, but the moment he's gone, I want it again. Always.

Chapter 12

Seth

"She's good?" Declan asks as he pulls away, leaning back in his seat and taking control of the polished steering wheel with one hand. Resting my head against the passenger side, I check the side-view mirror as the lights in my front room windows fade into nothing. The car jostles as Declan turns and hits the edge of a pothole.

"She's all right," I say, giving him a vague answer. I have to move, setting my elbow on the rest and letting my thumb tap against my bottom lip. She's not all right, but she's better. I know her and this isn't her. She's not addressing what I did, she's backing down from the fight. My babygirl doesn't pretend, and she doesn't hold things in. She's not all right. Something is wrong with her. Something's wrong with us and I don't know what.

"Are you good?"

"Tired and pissed." I answer him before looking at him. He knows I'm pissed. I haven't told him that I don't like that they left her in the cell with the hitman, but he doesn't need me to say it. I can read it on him and I'm sure he can tell I'm pissed just the same. Laura should have never been left in there. It was a calculated risk. And I hate them for it.

Declan is the spitting image of Carter, but with lighter hair, lighter eyes, and a more approachable personality. Every hard edge Carter has worked at having, Declan's cultivated the opposite. He wants people to come to him. He wants them to feel that they can trust him. It works.

"She's not bait." Apparently, I can't let it go. It's what irks me as I sit in this expensive sedan while Declan drives me away. They know I'm pissed. They know it was fucked. And yet, here I am, at war with an unknown man and pissed at the only allies I had.

"I know." Declan's tone is easy. He's always easy, but I've seen the way he handles situations. There's a grace about it, a calming air and then a brutal ending his opponent didn't see coming. It's all about the way he handles it, with both control and ease. "I told them that girl should have been taken out of Laura's cell the second she was placed in there."

The sun's only just peeking over the horizon, the pale pinks and oranges kissing at the edge of the skyline. Laura slept soundly for a little while, then woke up screaming again. He wants to know if she's all right? She's not. Part of the reason is because they let that situation occur. They could have stopped it. They didn't. And now she's not all right.

"She's not all right," Declan surmises. I only look at him in response, mute. "You can't hide it."

"How do you know that what I'm thinking is about her?"

"How could it not be about her?" he questions back. A deep ache settles in my chest and I have to look away.

"I can't stand this. She just had a hard time sleeping and now I'm leaving her. She woke up screaming, grabbing me. She has nightmares about it, Declan. She's not all right." He should know. They let that shit happen.

"She'll be all right," he answers. After a moment he adds, "She's strong... maybe it's better to be alone if she's doing that."

"Better to be alone?" I don't hide how I truly feel about his comment. How could he think that's better? Anger swims inside of me. He's the only friend I have out here. Him and his brothers. Yet here I am, wanting to beat their faces in.

He glances at me quickly, with confusion at first before explaining himself. "Well if she's grabbing you when you're sleeping... I was just thinking... you know, you react to that. Being grabbed in your sleep."

My head falls back and I stare at the visor and then up to the sunroof that still displays the fading night sky. "She's screaming, Declan. My first instinct is to find her." I explain it as calmly as I can remember something Declan told me that makes me feel like shit.

His first instinct isn't the same. I forgot about what he told me a year or more ago. That must be why he said what he did. Why he assumed her grabbing me wouldn't end well. And now I feel like shit. This edge I have needs to go. I need to get out this aggression before it gets me killed. Declan is not my enemy, even if I am pissed.

"Sorry," he says and adjusts his grip on the wheel, then looks out of his window, away from me. "I didn't mean for it to be taken like it was. It wasn't meant to be... cold."

"It's not," I say. "I get it." The streets are vacant as we drive. I'm quick to change subjects and put this to bed for now. "Everyone's going to be there?"

"The four of us. Daniel's staying back."

"Carter, Jase, you and me?" I question to clarify and Declan looks away to nod. I don't like it. I don't fucking like this one bit. Not when I'm pissed at them and they know it. "I'm not all right with the way things went down."

"We know," he answers and that's what causes the cold prick to travel down my back. I'm not comfortable against the leather. It's hot and this seat feels too small.

"If you knew I'd be pissed, then why?" I can't help but bite it out. "Why use her as bait?" They left her in there, hoping to get more information about who put the hit on her. I don't know how I could ever forgive them. Worse, I don't know how they'll react to knowing that.

"Carter got the note. It was never going to get to Jean." This is the first I'm hearing about it. I've been out for half a day now, and Declan's just now telling me?

"When?" I question and quickly spit out more. "What'd Marcus say in it? Where is it?"

"It's not Marcus. It's not his writing. Check the glove box," he says, reaching over. As the click of the lock fills the small cabin, he tells me, "We got it just after Walters gave Laura the package. If it had been delivered a moment before, things would've been different. I swear to you, if we'd already had the note, she'd have been in her own cell. She'd have been alone."

The small note is familiar; the type of paper, the handwriting. Marcus has a tell and these notes are it. It's his primary mode of communication. Thick handmade paper with deckle edges, his writing style, even how it's ripped. There's always a way to know it came from him and this looks like it did. My head spins reading it. Shock and fear come back with full force.

The note reads: *Make it quick. It's not her sin to pay.*

My veins freeze with the ice that courses through me. The need to rip it up, to crumble it, to smash my fisted hand against the window rides me hard. "He gave the order," I say and the tragic truth is ripped from me as my throat tightens and I read every word again. "She was going to die in there."

"Again, it's not Marcus. Someone wants it to look like him."

I stare at Declan for a moment, who gives nothing away, then back at the note. Bright lights from the streetlamps come and go, casting more illumination for me to see clearly.

"How the hell is this not Marcus?" I don't see it. It's everything we know that comes from him.

"Look at the tail ends of the letters, they're not like Marcus's handwriting. I put it through the system." Declan turns left, driving down a dirt road and past rural farms with bales of hay on either side of us. He explains, "It compares writing samples. This isn't from Marcus."

"What about the ones last week?" I can't help but to think back to the notes. The ones that convince me Marcus knows about my past.

"They're his." Declan's condolences are evident in his tone. "You ever decide on what you think it means?" he questions, taking a turn in the topic of conversation.

Which will it be? Fletcher's right-hand man? Or Laura's father?

"Did he want to kill them or did he have to..." I tell him the only conclusion I've come to. "I didn't want to kill Laura's father, but I had to. Fletcher was different. One was surviving this life, the other barely surviving life at all. I killed Fletcher for business. I killed Laura's father because I had to. Otherwise, I was dead and he'd have ended up dead too. There was no choice."

"Well, those were left by Marcus and obviously for you.

He's been following you, talking to you, but this last note wasn't from him. He didn't order a hit on Laura."

Thank fuck.

It's silent for a moment before I tell Declan, "It's a power play either way. He wanted me to know that he knew about me and Laura and what I'd done. He called my hand and I showed it."

"Anyone would have," Declan tells me like it's all right, but it's not.

"Everything's fucked because of it."

"I think you did something to piss Marcus off. He's creating problems for you."

"I haven't done anything worth him even noticing."

"It's the same shit that happened with Carter. Everything was an easy truce until he took Aria. We think it fucked with Marcus's plans, so he came for us."

"I didn't do anything though."

"If not you, then Laura," he tells me, meeting my gaze as we turn down a long dirt drive.

Anger consumes me at the mention of her name. "She's innocent in all of this and you know it." The threat is barely hidden in my tone.

"Delilah is still a factor. She has connections to Marcus and Laura knows her. We don't know what Marcus knows about the two of them or what he thinks Laura knows."

Rage pulses through me and I have to close my eyes.

"He didn't write the note though. He wants me to know he knows, but maybe he didn't send those guys to Laura's place."

"That's what I was thinking," Declan agrees. "Marcus is digging into your past. But someone else is going after you too. Someone who wants to pin it on Marcus."

"Walsh?" I question.

"No. No, not Walsh." The way he answers me, it's like he already knows.

"Who?"

As Declan puts the car into park, the dome lights giving off a soft glow inside the car, he smirks. "I think I know. I got a print."

"On the note?"

He only nods and continues. "And that print isn't in the system but it matches another print I took from Laura's place."

"One of the three pricks who broke in?"

"You are correct." Nodding, I crack my knuckles one at a time, peering outside. There's an old barn, the painted blue walls fresh compared to the wood on the doors, but still, it's worn down. Bright lights shine from inside the barn, and I make a note that there's nothing around here for miles and miles. Woods, and on the edge of the bay.

Another smirk shows first, followed by a grin. "I know you're pissed at me. But I have a gift for you."

Before I can respond, he turns off the car and slips out of the driver's door, leaving me there with apprehension. It only takes me a moment to get out, following him as he walks to the large sliding wooden doors to the barn.

Using both of his hands, he parts the opening and more light spreads across the field.

It's quiet, except for Jase's voice. "Took you long enough." I can barely hear him, walking a few paces behind Declan, but I know I heard him right.

I'm still rounding the front when I finally get a good look inside. The barn is at minimum twenty feet high and twenty feet across, but at least double that in length.

Carter and Jase stand side by side. Both cleanly shaven and each wearing slacks, black and gray respectively, and dress shirts. Carter's is rolled up to just above his elbows whereas Jase opted to keep his crisp white shirt sleeves down, complete with cuff links.

The two of them in this barn doesn't make sense. With the crowbars, hammer, and nail gun on a short wooden bench to their right, anyone could easily connect the dots.

They aren't the only ones waiting for us.

All three men are bound, on their knees, with burlap bags over their heads.

"Mine wasn't burlap," I comment, knowing in my gut these are the three fuckers who waited for me outside Laura's place. Their body types match up. My fingers itch with the need to rip the bags off their heads and make sure it's them.

Jase rolls his eyes and extends his hand to me as I follow

Declan to them. "You good?" he asks me, my hand firmly in his.

His prying gaze sinks deep into mine, searching for what I'm thinking.

"You know I'm pissed," I answer honestly, finally letting his hand go. His nod is nearly imperceptible, but then he tells me, "I would be too."

"You want to hit something," Carter speaks up and tilts his head to the man closest to him. "You can take it out on them."

Although it's not said in humor and it's not said casually, I know it's his attempt to ease the tension between us.

One of the men, the middle one, tries to say something, but he must be gagged because every loudly spoken word is muffled and the dumb fuck nearly falls forward on his face. He barely braces himself, still struggling to be heard.

"They say anything?" Declan asks, tossing his keys down next to the hammer and rolling up his sleeves. He takes them up inch by inch.

"That one is spilling everything," Jase answers him and gestures to the middle man. Of the men that night, I barely remember his figure. He's not the muscle, he's not the heavier one. He's the other guy. Inconsequential, but there. "The other two haven't given up shit."

"One may be a little hard to get to talk," Carter speaks up, flexing his hand and then crossing his arms. The knuckles on his right hand are split. "His jaw might be broken."

"Why'd you do that?" Declan says almost jokingly, making

his way to the line of silver tools on the bench. He's weighing a hammer in his right hand when Carter tells him the prick spit on him. "Anyone ever tell you that you have anger issues?" Declan says and then offers a smile as he holds up the hammer for me to see. Jase chuckles, Carter's still quiet and I shake my head in response to Declan's offer.

I haven't moved from my spot, unsure on what the plan is. Truth be told, I want them to myself. All three of them. They got to take out Davis. They shot him down, easily taking his life. I didn't get that justice. I haven't gotten anything. I wanted to hunt them down and take care of this myself. I don't want anyone else around when I take my anger out on each one of them, one at a time.

Although having them together, all at once does offer up a unique opportunity.

I want them to hear the sound of what happens when I'm crossed. I want the other two waiting and listening to their friend being beaten to death. It's fucked up and sick, but all I can wonder is what they were going to do to Laura. And every answer that comes into my head justifies beating them to death. And taking my time doing it.

"How's the gunshot?" Jase asks.

"All but forgotten about."

He nods and I catch Carter taking me in. "I've had worse and the bruise on my jaw is already letting up. I'll be fine," I answer them and I mean it. With everything going on, I haven't even thought about the gunshot. I take a pill in the morning for the pain, plus a pill in the evening. "Vicodin does wonders." My answer gets a laugh from Jase and Declan, not from Carter though.

Walking to the bench, I ask, "How'd you find them?"

With the doors still open, a breeze makes its way in and the faint smell of fresh water from the lake behind the barn comes with it.

The man in the middle leans forward, his shoulders shaking as he lets out a sob. A look of disgust plays on Carter's face.

"Middle man was the easy one. We had his license number from when we got Davis. It was linked to a credit card and that was linked to other bills, including an address."

Carter leans forward, ripping the bag off the man's head. His hair is matted on the right side, his face red and blotchy and a dingy rag spills from his mouth. He screams behind it, but the words are morphed into nothing that's identifiable.

His face, though, I recognize his face. "Yeah, that's one of them."

"He told us where the others were. It was easy enough to collect them."

Carter continues pulling off the bags and revealing the other two men. I didn't imagine I'd feel this much relief when I laid eyes on this crew again. It matches the animosity though.

I wanted an outlet for my aggression... here it is. Wrapped up in a pretty bow.

"He say anything interesting?" Declan asks and nods to the one in the middle. He shrieks behind the gag and that time I heard him. *Please.* He cried out please. It's muffled behind the rag, but I heard. I'm not going to give any mercy. He can scream whatever he wants to scream. He's as good as dead. The only consolation I have is knowing he'll regret ever stepping foot into Laura's apartment until the moment he dies.

"Yeah," Jase answers, leaning against the barn wall, propped up with his leg bent and one foot against the wall. "He said we're working with Walsh, and therefore we're free game."

"Free game?" Declan questions at the same time Carter huffs darkly, with true humor at the mention that the Cross brothers are *game*.

"Remove his gag, I'm sure he'll tell you we're as good as dead like he told us." Jase doesn't take his eyes off of him. His expression is empty of mercy and the man continues to beg. The other two men don't speak, they don't try to do a damn thing. One stares straight ahead while the other watches the four of us, focusing on whoever's speaking. He's the one with the broken jaw.

"Did you ask them why they went rogue?" I ask. That note is everything to me. The one made to look like Marcus's handwriting. I want to know why they did it. Why they decided to threaten Laura, to take her life, and why pin it on Marcus by writing the note the way they did.

"With the note?" Jase asks to clarify.

"Yeah," I say as my voice hardens and I have to shove my hands in my jean pockets just to keep from reaching out to them. "One of them wrote it, right?"

Carter kicks the back of the man seated directly in front of him, the one staring straight ahead.

"We didn't ask. You should though," he informs me. "His print is on it."

Every step is careful as I move toward the man. He's in blue slacks and a collared shirt, almost like a uniform. He's the tallest of the three. I crouch down in front of him, but an arm's length away and rip the gag from his mouth, tossing it into the dirt. No matter how hard of a man he wants to appear, he still retches from the cloth being removed. He spits on the ground at my feet and I wait, letting the anger pass. I need to know: was it just them, or was Marcus involved in any way at all? I have to know who all of my enemies are.

"Why'd you want to pin murdering my girl on Marcus? Did he send you to her house?" I ask and when the prick doesn't answer, I add, "He's pissed about Walsh, so he goes after a woman? That doesn't seem like Marcus."

Silence.

"Seems like something a dickless coward would do. There's no way a man like Marcus would go after someone's girl. You want to be Marcus, but you aren't." My last line triggers something.

The man's eyes flash for a moment and he clenches and

unclenches his jaw, still not saying anything. I don't mean to do it, at least I'm not conscious of it, when I strike out and slam my fist into his nose.

"Fuck!" the man screams and leans backward, which only makes him fall. The blood from his broken nose leaks into the dirt, and Jase lets him lie there for only a moment before forcing him back to his knees. All the while he fights it. I shake out my hand, reeling inside. I need to know. I have to know who wanted her dead. Every name. Every single name involved. They all have to die.

"Look guys, he's not mute," I say, deadpan. "For a moment, I thought I was having a one-sided conversation." Everything on the outside of me, is at odds with what's going on internally. Even the control. I need them to talk, to tell me what happened, or else I have nothing. They're on their knees, at my mercy, but I still have nothing.

The middle man speaks up again, his eyes wide and his words muffled. Both men on his left and right glare at him.

I rip the cloth out of his mouth. "You have something you want to share?" *Please. Please*, I pray, *give me something. Tell me what happened that led to this.*

"Please, I'll tell you everything, just let me go."

"No." My answer is immediate and the man's eyes dilate as they go wide. He's hit with shock at first. He'll still tell me. I know he will. I have to believe that; I need him honest in his final hours. *I'll be honest too, just tell me.*

"We told them it was up to you," Carter informs me. "Guess he was hopeful that you would have mercy."

"Please!" he begs, his single word yelled in such a high pitch it breaks from his throat being dry. "I'll tell you everything. Anything you want to know."

"You think you could do that? And then you could leave here and Marcus wouldn't kill you?" Tears leak from the man's eyes. "If you could do that, then whatever you have to say isn't worth enough to even hear it."

"It is! Marcus is leaving. He's not going to be here. Please! I can tell you everything."

My gaze shifts to Carter, who's looking at Jase. A chill creeps into the silent room as the man heaves in air. "It was a mistake. I just want out! I want out of it all!"

The man who wrote the note, the one with the print on the letter, he curses in what I think is Russian before heaving his body at the middle man, his teeth sinking into the man's cheeks and blood gushes from it. It's not too deep, merely a gash, but blood leaks freely and the middle man screams out in agony, toppling over. I don't make an attempt at all to stop it. I want chaos, I want them to attack each other. In violence there's truth.

Carter grabs the first man by the back of his shirt, forcefully righting him and the man spits once again at the dirt under the middle man's feet. A tinge of his blood remains.

Standing up, I walk backward, assessing the scene in

front of me. One man on his knees, glaring at the rat he used to work with, blood staining his mouth. The middle one wriggling on the dirt, his cheek slashed. The third still only watches, the one with the broken jaw, hanging lower than it should on the right side. All I need to know, is which of these three will tell me the truth.

"Marcus is leaving?" Declan asks Jase before I can. Carter stays where he is behind the three men, glaring at them and waiting. He's a brooding man and silent. Jase tilts his head for Declan and me.

"He said earlier, Marcus is picking a successor." He's not whispering, but he's not speaking loud enough for the men on their knees to hear us. A successor? He choosing someone to take his role?

"He's condoning going after women?" The disgust in my voice is evident.

"He gave a list of ways to prove themselves. It's up to his nominations to execute them."

"Free rein to do whatever they want to prove themselves," Carter says and Jase nods, agreeing with him. "That's what it looks like." Marcus told them he's leaving, and that whoever proves himself worthy, can take his place.

"Free rein?" I question, needing answers and not knowing who will have them. "My name was on a list, and they decided to involve Laura? Or was she included in the free-for-all?"

"Just you," the middle man whimpers out the answer that

gives me my first bit of peace.

Although anxious heat sweeps across my shoulders and chest, the knowledge that Marcus isn't going after us, after Laura and me together, is a relief I didn't dream of having. Maybe he is still coming after me and he's digging into my past, but Laura isn't in his sights. She's safe. She *should* be safe. These fuckers will pay the price for dragging her into this hell.

"Which one of them decided that Laura would pay? Which one?" I speak up loud enough for everyone to hear, my last question coming out harder. "Marcus sent his men out to prove themselves, and one of you decided to hurt her." The men are silent, and I look past them at Carter. "I want him. I want the man who decided she needed to die." He gets that price on his head for his print being on the note. I don't even know if he made the call, but he's the one I'll take care of last.

"You can have them all," Carter answers, bringing all three of us to stare back at him. The middle man is back on his feet, his head hung low.

I eat up the space that separates us from them, leaving Declan and Jase behind me. Gripping the man who tells every secret, I drag him up to me by the collar until we're face to face.

"I'm going to ask you a simple question." He's already nodding his head, eager to tell me whatever I want to hear as I ask, "Did Marcus tell you to go after Laura?"

"No. He didn't. It was Jared's idea. He said it would send you on a spiral downward."

"Is that one Jared?" I nod to my left and even though Carter's nodding behind the man in my grasp, he answers quickly. "Yes, and that's his brother," he adds, motioning with his head which is the only thing he can move.

I drop the man, letting him fall to the ground.

"They just needed me to drive... I shouldn't have been there. I shouldn't have done it. I knew I shouldn't have," the man bawls.

"Jared goes last," I announce, feeling strangely calm considering the amount of hate that's fueling my decisions.

"Whatever you want. This is our apology," Carter announces and as fucked up as it is, I answer, "Apology accepted."

I take the gun out of its holster and weigh it in one hand and then the other.

"I've been trying to decide... if I should shoot you first, since you gave up everything so easily." The man in the middle looks hopeful for a moment, although he still shakes his head. My tone when I speak again clues him in to what I'm thinking before I crouch down in front of him, both hands on the gun between my legs. "The thing is, I don't trust you. So I can't give you that mercy."

"No! No! I told you all everything!" He's still pleading when I nod at Jase and he picks up the gag, shoving it back into the man's mouth. Chaos swarms him, but it dies down easily, settling into hopelessness.

"Him first, I think." I speak out loud and the three

brothers nod in unison. He can't speak so it makes sense to get rid of him first.

"I have another question," I mention as the thought hits me. "Who sent her flowers?"

The look Jase gives me is unexpected, but Declan knows what I'm referring to. "Who was it?" I harden my voice, and the man in the middle mentions a single name.

Marcus. He told me that Marcus said she deserved a warning, another beginning to an end.

I do exactly what I pictured when I first saw them here. I don't use a single item from the line of silver metal. I opt for my fists. It's brutal and taxing on my body. It takes a lot to beat a man to death. After the first one, I have to take off my shirt; it's covered in sweat and blood and I'm so damn hot.

Middle man must've been speaking the truth because he was still pleading for his life, giving the same information over and over again until his windpipe collapsed under my knuckles.

The man who wrote the note, the one responsible for all the pain my babygirl went through, he goes last and before the second man hit the dirt dead, the bitch was crying, begging me.

Every man will break. Some are easier than others.

All three of them stay, watching and helping me when I ask them to.

I can't go home when it's over, since I'm covered in blood and angry. I'm still raw and wound up and the cuts on my hand have worsened and split. Declan takes me back to the estate instead, leaving Carter and Jase to clean up the mess. She's got work in only an hour anyway. That's how long it took. I can't let her see this shit right before she leaves and has normalcy. I can't drop this burden on her.

Declan's quiet until we park. "What are you going to do with Laura?" Declan's question catches me off guard and I don't like it. He should know better than to even say her name right now.

"What do you mean?" I'm fucking exhausted and I don't have time to decipher what he's getting at.

"Last time I asked you, you said you didn't know."

What am I going to do with her? "I'll do right by her. Get her a ring when all this settles." Declan nods at my simple answer and I find myself doing the same. I'm going to love her. That's all I can do and it's what she deserves. I'll do anything and everything that she wants. It's an easy answer, but every one of my thoughts stays bottled up. He knows about the ring, he knows she's mine, and that should be good enough. Everything else is just for me and Laura. It's only for us.

"And she's good with that?" The car is still running and the headlights shine into the woods. I focus on the lights.

"I think so." Declan's quiet but he's watching me. I can feel his eyes on me. Swallowing, I tell him, "She leaves when things get rough and this life is rough." I think about telling him that if she wants to go, away from here, away from this life, I'm out. So I do. I lay it out for him, and he accepts it. As if he saw it coming.

He's silent, but nods in understanding. His jaw is hard though, his brow pinched.

"So you two are good?" he asks again. Prying and the more he asks, the more I find myself telling.

"I don't know how to set boundaries with her. Every time I try, it goes wrong, everything falls apart, things get worse." It's her running away from *me*. I don't know how to stop it. "She can't leave me. She needs to know that's not an option."

It takes a long moment of silence before Declan answers me, "She doesn't strike me as a woman who likes boundaries."

"She's mine. And she needs to understand that."

He throws his hands up and says, "I didn't say that she didn't. Some women... they aren't submissive." His grip on the wheel gets a little tighter, his voice a little harder before he leans back, forcing himself to relax.

There's an edge to him. Declan's never had a woman he loved, as far as I know. He has needs though and I know he goes to this place, a club of sorts. He has experience in that way. But he doesn't have experience with loving someone. He doesn't know Laura at all.

"I like submissive. I need that control, you know."

"Yeah."

"You love her, and she's not submissive—"

"You haven't seen her in that way," I cut him off. Laura

likes it when I take control. I know she does.

"In the topping from the bottom in bed kind of way? I'm sure I don't need to see it to know it."

"I'm sure as fuck not the submissive if that's what you're getting at."

"It doesn't work like that. I'm just saying, maybe she needs control as much as you do. You two work. I've seen it. You love each other. That's enough, man. You don't need to force her to agree to boundaries that have hurt her before. It'll happen when it's supposed to. Let her have the control she needs, and you might be surprised."

"I'm just afraid she's going to leave me." I speak the honest truth. I've had this with her before. It's the only thing I want. The only thing worth living for. "If I lose her again..." my voice trails off and I have to look away.

"You won't," Declan tells me confidently. It's only then I can meet his gaze. He nods, and adds, "You aren't going to lose her. You two are meant for each other. Nothing's going to come between that."

He sounds so sure, so confident, that I believe him because that's what I want to do. I want to believe I'll have her forever.

Chapter 13

Laura

"You aren't supposed to be here," Aiden says. The amount of irritation he grits out in his comment is enough to make me roll my eyes, which I do since my back is both to him and the door to the back office. "I'm serious, Laura, you shouldn't be back until you're given the okay."

I hear him, but I'm not listening as I shelve the thick binder of medical records.

"It's a mandatory leave." His voice hardens when I ignore him, opting to continue exactly what I'm doing instead.

I am needed here and I'll be damned if I'm going to let him send me away. Melody's been transferred while she awaits trial. She's not here anymore, which I'm silently grateful for, but I have paperwork to transfer. Early yesterday morning,

I left jail. This morning, I'm back at work. I don't see the problem, just a striking difference in scenery.

"Laura, are you going to make me call security?" he asks with exasperation and my answer is just the same.

"No. I'm sticking to my schedule." I guess the saving grace in all of this is that I didn't miss a shift. I want normalcy and this is the easiest way to get that.

His relief is palpable as he sighs and says, "Please just stay home for the week."

I turn to him, my ponytail swinging and the tips of my hair tickle my shoulder as I look him in the eyes and tell him, "No. You aren't calling security and I'm staying."

"We're doing an internal investigation, for fuck's sake," he practically hisses beneath his breath. The door's still open and Bethany takes the opportunity to walk in.

Thank the Lord for her. I thought her shift would never start.

"You're back," she says brightly, oblivious to Aiden's irritation and I return her smile, but mine's thin-lipped and cut off by Aiden.

"No, she's not."

"Yes, I am."

"We need her." If Aiden sounded exasperated, then Bethany sounds desperate. Grabbing both sides of the threshold to the small room, she leans in and whispers harshly to Aiden, whose hand is currently running down his face. "Cindy isn't good for a damn thing."

"I know," I stress to Bethany, giving Aiden the cold shoulder. "How did she even get through her boards?"

He may be my boss, but I'll be damned if he's going to keep me away. Especially given the activity he's been involved with around here.

"There's an investiga—"

"Over the woman with only initials?" I question him. "Over her being in here with limited information and files? Or over what happened when she had to have emergency surgery?"

He pales and when he speaks his voice is so dry, he has to swallow and then try again. "This is about you."

"If you push this, I'll push too." It hurts me, truly and deeply to look my boss in the eyes, a man I respect and make that threat. I don't know what he's up against, but he doesn't know what I'm dealing with either. Bethany's silent and I see her shrink back, but she doesn't leave. Maybe due to curiosity, maybe she wants to serve as moral support.

"Laura, this isn't about—"

"I don't care what it's about, I'm not leaving." My throat squeezes and I feel hot all over as I hug the binder to my chest. They can't make me go. Work is my life and the only thing that makes me feel good right now. "I need to be helping someone," I plead with him.

"We have to. It's procedure."

"Then she doesn't have to check in," Bethany pipes up.

She looks nervously at me before meeting Aiden's gaze. "She can be here unofficially. You know we need the help, so as long as it's not documented..." She leaves the sentence unfinished and the two of us stare at Aiden.

He's cornered. Figuratively and literally. His answer is a very quickly spoken *fine* before he leaves. He's pissed and I get it. Everything around here is falling to hell.

"I'm so glad you're back," Bethany says and takes a step in as I stack another binder on top of the one I've already placed on the desk. Bethany sits on the edge of it before asking, "Seth all right?"

I nod, my voice suddenly lost. It's easy to stand up to Aiden, since he doesn't know everything. Bethany knows it all though. When you call someone early in the morning or late at night, and you lose your shit over the phone, it can be hard to look them in the eye the next morning. That's what it feels like right now.

"I still haven't seen him, though." My voice nearly cracks and I pause my motions, holding a binder that isn't the right one and slowly but surely, resting my head against the shelf. "He hadn't come home before I left." I called her when I woke up alone. I spilled every detail.

Except the part about my heart. And the part about Jean.

I told her enough that she knows I'm not okay. And that Seth and I were fighting. It's enough for her to understand. There's so much going on and everything feels like it's coming to a head.

I want to tell her about my heart, but not yet.

I'm not telling anyone until after the appointment confirms it. I just... I just have to make sure I don't skip the appointment. Which means Seth's men will follow me, but at least they're only following. They won't know why.

"Did you call him, though?" she asks and I only shake my head, feeling the swoosh of my hair before getting back to the binders.

I don't answer her question. Instead I confess the conclusion I arrived at after I spilled my guts on the phone to her and sat there alone in a quiet room with nothing to do but think. That's really what drove me to work. I couldn't be alone with my thoughts.

"Even if I called him, I don't know what I would say."

"Every couple has that moment," Bethany says with slight dejection. When she shifts on the desk she opens the binder. The telltale creak is the only reason I know she did. "I think getting to that moment is the start of something better. That's what I think."

"When did you become an optimist?" I question, pursing my lips when I find the last binder and turn to finally look her in the eyes.

With her hair up in a messy bun, she shrugs. "I like your scrubs though," she comments and I have to utter a small laugh. We're wearing matching *I love my patients a latte* scrubs with little coffee cups all over them.

"You have good taste," I tell her, closing the binder she was absently fiddling with and placing the third on top.

"I'm glad you're back. You're never allowed to leave me again," Bethany says and pouts. Literally sticking out her bottom lip, which makes me laugh a bit louder than the last time.

"Love you more than coffee," I tell her, placing a quick kiss on her cheek and slipping out of the room as she moves to find whatever it was that she needed. She calls out to my back, "Me too, but don't make me prove it."

It's nice to smile. It occurs to me that this is the first time I've smiled in days when I'm back at the nurses' station, pulling out the file numbers and testing a pen on a sticky note before opening up the binder to fill out the first bit of information.

"Do you have a pen for the sign-in sheet please?" a feminine voice asks and I peek up. Plastering on a smile, I answer her, "Right here," and pass her my pen that I know works, opting to grab another.

"Thank you." With the thinning of her gray hair, the woman's much older and I think I recognize her as the mother of one of our residents who's in and out. She's the mom who smiles to everyone's face but cries behind closed doors and at the back of empty halls. Even when you find her there, she'll smile and say she's all right, when in reality she's breaking inside.

I know her type and I feel for her.

"Have a good day," she tells me kindly, setting the pen down and taking in a deep breath as she prepares to go down one of the far halls. They aren't my residents down that hall. We're sectioned off but I watch her go, wishing there was a different way. It hurts to feel helpless, even more so when someone you love is in pain or a situation that's hurting them and they don't know how to get out.

She wore a dress and rouge for the occasion. Some call that lipstick courage.

I retrieve my pen, since the next one I try doesn't work and it goes straight to the trash bin under the counter.

The second I drop my gaze to the paperwork, a splash of blond hair catches my eye. The elevators are closing and the woman is off to one side of it, but a familiar chill spreads through me. Recognition mixed with fear and regret flows through my veins.

My lips part as a breath leaves me and I drop the pen, moving to the side of the desk in an attempt to get a better look.

Cami.

I swear it's Cami.

The doors close before I can fully see her and my deranged self decides to take the stairs, nearly running down the hall to get to the stairwell and therefore her, before she can leave. *It's Cami.* That's my only thought the entire way to the stairs even though I know she's dead. It can't be her. It's not possible, but I *feel* like it is. I can feel *her.* As I wrap my hand around the railing, taking each step as quickly as possible, I argue with my sound mind that it's Cami. There is no logical explanation, but there's a feeling when someone you know and love deeply comes close to you. You can feel them and it's her. I know it's her.

"Excuse me." I'm breathless as I give the apology, nearly bumping into an orderly as I round the last set and swing myself into the door. I pry it open in just enough time to see her leaving. A gust of wind blows her hair to the side as she slips out of the front doors across the room.

Her name is trapped in the back of my throat as my heart races. Just as the doors close, I call out, "Cami!"

The receptionist stares at me. She's the only one here and she stands awkwardly as I run past her.

Hustling to get across the reception area, I make my way while avoiding the prying eyes of the receptionist and whatever she's saying and slam my hands into the door, forcing it open. It's cold and unforgiving; the leaves have all changed color seemingly overnight. The sky is gray and the parking lot is empty. Wrapping my arms around myself, I walk down the front stairs, searching for her.

I even call out her name again. As I stand there all alone in the cold, I realize it's the first time I've said her name out loud in years. Years.

There are no people, no cars, no lights or sign that anyone is out here.

It's like she disappeared.

"Are you all right?" the receptionist asks me from behind.

"Of course," I answer her with my head lowered and look up one last time down the empty sidewalk and then to the parking lot.

"Do you need me to call security or help?" she offers and I only shake my head. Asking her if she recognized the woman proves she doesn't. She hadn't seen her come in and didn't get a good look at her when she left.

When I get back to the nurses' station, still feeling the cold blistering my cheeks, I check the log for visitors, and I recognize most of them. There are no new names on the sign-in sheet and no one named Cami.

She was here though; I know she was.

Chapter 14

Seth

The front door opens with a soft creak. It could have been silent and Laura still would've heard. She's waiting for me.

"Where were you?" The accusation is out of her mouth before she can even lift her head from the back of the sofa to glare at me.

Guilt-ridden, I close the door behind me and toss the keys onto the entryway table.

"With Jase and Declan."

She grabs the remote from next to her and taps it against her thigh, an agitated sigh leaving as she does.

"I didn't mean to be gone so long." I tell her before she can yell at me, "I felt like shit leaving you here." I felt like shit there, which is why I took so long. The meds work for pain, but I fell apart the moment I sat down at the estate. Sleep and an IV proved useful for getting me back on my feet. I could have done that here, though. Next time, I will.

She doesn't respond, but her gaze softens at least.

"How are you doing?" I ask as I take each step to her with careful intention.

"Okay... Work was fine," she answers, flicking off the television in the middle of a scene. If I had to guess, she wasn't invested in it. Licking her lower lip, she stares at her socks as she pulls her legs into her chest. "How long have you been home?"

"Two hours. I couldn't sleep."

"You want me home when you sleep?" I ask her, needing to come up with a solution before she can even finish the complaint. She nods, her chin nestled against her knees. "If I'm not allowed to leave, you should at least be here."

"I know," I agree and fall onto the sofa, wrapping my arm around her and pulling her in. "I know. I'm sorry." The second she settles her head onto my chest, I kiss the crown of her head. She's still got her arms hugging herself and is in a huddled ball, but at least she doesn't seem to be angry. Pulling her in closer, I tell her, "I had a difficult time this morning and it lasted a few hours. I had to decompress for a moment and when I did, I realized I lost track of time."

"Where?" Her question isn't spoken lightly. "You couldn't decompress here?"

"I was pretty worked up," I answer her although I'm hiding a lot of it. I'm still angry. More than angry. The three of those men could die a thousand deaths and they'd still deserve more. The anger I can push down, but damn was I worn out. I felt like death. The doc told me I shouldn't be pushing it like that, but I have to do what I have to do.

"You can be worked up and still come home," she says and her tone is less pissed off and more pleading as she peeks up at me. "There's beer in the fridge."

Before she can look away, back to the blank television screen, I grab her chin between my thumb and forefinger and plant a quick kiss against her lips. "Thank you."

Her eyes stay closed for a long moment and she asks before she opens them, "For what?"

"For not being too mad."

A sad smile graces her lips. "I don't want to fight. I'm finding it hard to be mad these days."

I don't care for how she says it. It shifts something inside me although I don't know why. "I got you a gift." I wasn't going to tell her but seeing her like this, I had to say something to make the smile turn genuine.

"What is it?"

"It comes in the mail, so you have to wait." The answer makes me feel like an ass and when she rolls her eyes, that makes it worse. "It's flowers. Every two weeks, flowers will come in the mail."

"Really?" The interest in her voice and the sweet blush on her cheeks make it worth it.

"Really." I add, "They had options for the kinds you like and I picked the wildflower type and roses too. I know you like a mix, but you always smile at the roses too."

With sleep in her eyes, her hair still damp from a shower and wearing nothing but my t-shirt and a pair of short shorts for bed, Laura looks up at me and instead of saying a word, she steals a kiss.

It's quick and in return I give her a smile; the kind you feel in your chest. That's all I want. That warmth in my chest, that love from her. It's fucking everything.

"Better?" I ask, feeling the weight of the world leave my shoulders.

"A little." She bristles and adds, "I still don't like being alone here."

Rubbing my neck with my free hand, the one not wrapped around her waist, I answer her, "I know. It won't happen often. And you'll like it here more when you move your things in."

I anticipate her arguing based on her initial reaction, judging from the small gasp of protest that leaves her and the way her lips part, but she hesitates and then closes her mouth, opting for a small nod. "Yeah," she says, stretching forward and then standing. "You're right. I need to move my things in." Her tone drops, as does her gaze.

I don't know what to make of her reaction. Something's wrong and off and I don't know what. She isn't right. "You sure you're okay?"

"Fine," she says as gets up.

As she makes her way to the kitchen, I see she's spackled the wall over the hole I punched in it. She cleaned up and that spackle is the only evidence left of anything that started our recent downfall. I hate the numbing prick that climbs over me at the memory of it. I'll paint it in the morning, getting rid of any evidence at all. Maybe that's it. Maybe that's what made her react like that.

"You want a beer?" Laura asks me and when I move my gaze to her, I get a full-on view of her sweet curves as she bends down, opening the fridge and taking out a bottle of ginger ale in one hand and a beer in the other, holding it up in offering.

"Yeah," I answer, readjusting on the sofa. She could do anything, anything at all and it would be sexy as fuck. But offering me a beer in short shorts has to be at the top of my fantasy list now. "No wine?" I question her as she closes the door with her hip.

"My stomach is messed up. But I've got it when I'm ready for a glass." Her tone is flat and sleep weighs down her eyes. With the ice tinkling against her glass, she sits back down, sipping her drink and passing me my beer.

It's quiet as we both have a drink in silence. I fucking hate the odd tension between us. "Are we okay?"

"What?" She's confused at first and I simply wait for her to answer. "Yeah, we are."

"I just want to feel like we're okay and something... I want to see you happy."

"You're sweet." She smiles up at me, squeezing my hand. "When did that happen?"

"Guess you're rubbing off on me."

"I don't feel sweet."

I lean down to kiss her, just once, a small peck, but keep my nose touching hers. "Still taste sweet," I whisper against her lips. All I'm rewarded with is a small smile that doesn't last long. "I know things are off right now, but give it time. Everything will be better. I promise."

"You're making a lot of promises," she says and her voice is soft, low, and full of doubt. Doubt that wouldn't be there if we were as good as she keeps saying we are.

"And I aim to keep every one of them, Babygirl." That nickname does it every time. Her eyes light up, her lips turn up, everything goes up and everything is better when I call her *Babygirl*.

It's only a flicker though and then she falls back into this state she's in... It drives me crazy.

"Tell me what's wrong. Tell me now," I demand.

"I just really want to go back to what we were. What we had, you know?" she asks me and the sincerity, the desperation is too much. Her voice cracks and she closes her eyes as she adds, "Can we just pretend to go back and never go through all of this?" She opens her eyes when I don't answer and says, "I just want to go back to the very beginning. Back to you being on my porch steps."

"I never left." I answer her with all that I have. If that's what she wants, she can have it and more. There's an emptiness that she used to fill. Even when I didn't have her, I could still feel her there. She's slipping again. I can feel it but I don't know why.

Her response is somber as she sets down the glass in her hand. "Right, I'm the one who fucked that up."

"Hey, don't do that. I'm just saying, I never stopped..." I trail off although the words *loving you* are there. Right there, but I still can't say it. Not when I feel like there's something between us and I don't know what it is. "I was always *yours*," I stress. "Whatever else I am in this life won't ever hold a candle to that flame. I'm nothing if you're not there, so I pretend you're waiting for me at that door. It's how I got through it and I never left. In my head I was always there, so close to seeing you again."

I don't anticipate her crying. She's not one to be so emotional but the last few days have been heavy and I wish I could find a way to make it right. Fuck, I'm trying. I'm trying to hold us together and failing. As quickly as I can, I wrap my arm around her but she pulls back, resisting me.

Her words are muffled angrily. "You can't say things like that."

"Like what?" *What the fuck did I do?*

"Like your only good side is me, and that you being with me is…"

"What's wrong with that?" The beer bottle clanks on the coffee table as I set it down. It's exasperating; I don't even know why we're fighting right now. We should be good. She keeps saying we are but we aren't.

"You aren't leaving me, right? Because it sure as hell feels like you are." Panic stricken. As I sit here, I am panic stricken and helpless. When did I become so helpless?

"I asked you to hold me until the end, right?" she asks and her voice gets tight. "That's all I want. It's my only wish right now. I just want you to hold me."

"Then why are you so sad? I've never seen you like this. I can feel that things aren't right."

She falls forward, her head in her hands and this time when I try to hold her, she lets me. Something is off. Something's so wrong and I can feel it. I know there's something she's hiding.

"Tell me what's wrong," I whisper and then add, "I'll fix it. I promise."

"I just want you to hold me, Seth."

"I'm so fucking sorry," I tell her with a ragged voice. I can't control the emotion inside of me. It's screaming that I'm losing her even though she's telling me the opposite. "What can I do? Just tell me; I'll do it."

Seeing her like this wrecks me. She's not supposed to be sad like this and broken. "I hate myself for putting you through this."

"It's not your fault," she says and shakes her head, even as the tears fall.

"It is my fault. It's all my fault and I'm so damn sorry."

She does the opposite of what I expect. She climbs into my lap and holds me. Her arms are around my neck and her head rests in the crook of it. "I love you, Seth King. I love you."

Hearing her whisper that calms me, but only slightly. So long as she's hurting, I won't be all right and it only forces the aggression to build.

"With nothing to fix, what can I do?"

"Just hold me."

My phone goes off at fucking 4:00 a.m. Laura's asleep in the crook of my arm and the insistent buzzing won't stop. My eyes are burning from the lack of sleep, but I scrub them with one hand as I slip Laura onto her pillow. She wouldn't let go of me. She won't tell me anything else either.

I've never felt so helpless with her.

I'm groggy as fuck and I can barely see as I make my way out of the bedroom and answer the phone although I don't actually listen to whoever's on the other end yet.

It's pitch black in my hallway but the second I get to the living room, the lights from the porch make getting to the kitchen counter easy enough. I lean on it and hear the muted "You there?" from the other end of the line.

"I'm here," I breathe into the phone, finally lifting it to my ear.

"Are you listening?"

"I am now," I answer Declan and take in a deep inhale, my eyes still half lidded as I lean against the counter. "What's going on?"

"You said Walsh told you he looked into you and Laura?" he questions.

"Yeah." I perk up slightly at Declan's tone, but I need strong black coffee if I'm going to make it through this. "What's going on?" It's hard to shut off the thoughts about Laura and just focus. I can't get over this nagging feeling that everything is wrong.

"There's no alert, Seth." My eyes open at what Declan just told me, staring at the coffee maker with the mug in my hand.

"Walsh said he didn't know about Laura and me until recently." I repeat the conflict out loud, "But you don't have an alert that he searched my name?"

"Right." He adds before I can ask, "Or Laura's."

"So go farther back with the dates on the system."

"I did that already. I searched for a month. Bethany was

curious about you, by the way."

That part doesn't strike me as odd. I bet she hates me for putting Laura through all of this too. So long as she doesn't tear her away from me, she can hate me all she wants. That makes two of us.

"Check his work computers. The computers that aren't registered. Maybe it looks like someone else."

"No. No one looked up Laura other than Bethany until Laura was arrested. Not a soul. I wanted to do the search to see if we got any hits. There's no search for her or any information regarding you that included her." I'm silent, still trying to process what all this means and Declan keeps talking.

"It hit me a bit ago that Walsh told you he did. He said he looked you up. I never got an alert. He's lying."

"Could have been a paper trail?" I ask although that's unlikely. A chill runs down my arms as I hit the button to brew a pot of coffee. Why would he lie about something like that? It doesn't make sense.

"No. I looked into the police transcripts in your hometown. Nothing has been moved or requested."

"Either he already knew or he figured it out without searching online, and if that's the case, who did he talk to?"

"We have eyes on all our men. We've had eyes on Walsh. He hasn't seen anyone."

"I know. No one who knows would have told him shit." I don't know what to make of it all.

He tells me firmly from the other end of the phone, "My instinct is that he's lying. I think he knew about you and Laura all along. He went to her work, he befriended her."

"So he's playing us?" I can practically see Declan nodding the way that he does before he says, "Yes."

"And to think I'd just started to come around to him."

"You're a liar. You don't like that prick." I huff a short chuckle at Declan's response. Bringing the coffee to my lips, I take a long sip before asking, "So what do we do about it?"

"That's why I'm calling you. I thought you'd want to take the lead on this. Get ahead of it."

"Another gift?" I question and make my way to the sofa, taking a seat. Before he can answer, I tell him, "I told you, apology accepted, it's all behind me."

It's quiet for a moment before he asks, "You sure?" Thinking back to the barn, I flex my hand and then crack my knuckles.

"I'm sure."

"Still," he says on the other end of the line, "what do you want to do about Walsh?"

"He knows more than he's letting on. We all do. We keep our cards close. I don't trust him and I want him gone as quickly as we can get him out of here." I think out loud, "Marcus is supposedly leaving, maybe Walsh goes with him. I don't want anything to do with either of them."

"They both have their sights set on you. The question is, why?"

Chapter 15

Laura

Life is an oddity when you're waiting to see a doctor who is, more than likely, going to inform you that your death is coming shortly. The days blur together because every so often time pauses while you remember, and then it goes on, but in the back of your mind you're caught in that thought.

It's a constant. I can't shake it and it's wearing away at me. To the point where I made the damn appointment, even though I'd rather just hide. I'd rather pretend I don't know that I have heart failure. Apparently I'm shit at pretending.

"Hey, it's just a checkup," Bethany says sweetly beside me and I smile as she pats my shoulder. She does a little circle with her hand and then pats me once more in finality.

"Haven't you ever heard, doctors make the worst

patients... and nurses aren't much better," I joke back at her, forcing myself to be the person she knows me to be. That's the way I've been with Seth too. I think they both see through it. I wish I was a better liar for their sake.

The waiting room is virtually empty. It's just us in the back row of these rather uncomfortable seats, closest to the magazines. There's a pregnant woman a row up. She's been on her phone the entire time; her hand is rubbing circles over her belly. It's calming to watch.

A single laugh is belted out by Bethany in response and then she flips the page to her magazine. "Speaking of that, I need to schedule a checkup too."

"Ooh, hypocritical much?" I taunt her.

The magazine makes a slapping sound as she tosses it down on her lap. "You look like you're going to an executioner, not a doctor."

My smile falls and it happens so fast and honestly that I don't have time to correct it.

"Hey," she says and her voice falls gently as she leans in, her hand on my thigh. "You okay?"

"I'm fine," I lie and at that moment my heart sputters, like it's scolding me for doing so. I have to clear my throat and pick up my coffee, which is the cue for her to remove her hand. "Just a lot on my mind." It's a lame excuse, but Bethany buys it.

"It's Seth, isn't it?"

"What?" The word is only a single breath. I can't even

take a sip of the coffee. Why would she think it's Seth?

"You used to tell me everything. Literally five months ago, you described the worst date with at least decent consolation sex. You've been with Seth for like... weeks? And you haven't told me anything."

"It's been almost a month," I say, correcting her. "He's not like the other guys. This isn't a one-off to have drinks over and laugh at. He's not a date... he's... he's more."

"But you aren't happy," she emphasizes.

I'm happy with him. I don't know how to tell her how wrong she is. "I've changed and I know that, but it's not because of Seth. I promise you."

"If you don't want to be with him, don't. He can't force you—"

"I love him," I say, cutting her off. I'm not angry at her; I'm shocked, though. "I've always loved him and even though..." I trail off because I don't even know where to start. Our love story isn't a straight line, it's chaotic scribbles on a page. It's fucked up. "I need him right now. Why would you question that?"

"You haven't seemed right. Something's going on," she presses and I don't know what to tell her. I can't tell her the truth. I can't tell anyone. Not yet. I can't make it real for them like it is for me.

"Will you give me some time?" I ask her. "I just need time to figure it all out."

Her smile is small but genuine, and I get another pat too. "Of course." As she's telling me, "All the time you need," a nurse calls out my name.

"All righty," she says then stands with me and tells me she'll see me at work. I hate that I'm lying to her and to Seth, or at least lying by omission to hide the truth. I make a promise to myself as I watch her go before handing the papers to the nurse, that I'll tell them. I'll tell both of them everything the moment this appointment is done.

I can't keep lying and pretending.

"Miss Roth?" The doctor is short like me, although her shoes add at least two inches. *Cheater.* "Right this way." She's professional but walks quickly, as if she's in a hurry. It only makes me more anxious. She doesn't speak the entire way to the room, which is in the farthest corner of this place, adding yet again to my anxiousness.

"I'm Doctor Tabor."

"Hi, it's nice to meet you." Formalities take precedence although internally all I can think is that it is not, at all, nice to meet her.

"I see you've already had your blood taken?" she questions and I nod, my fingers drifting on the small bandage in the crook of my arm.

"I don't know why it was necessary." I didn't ask the nurse when she told me. I was too busy talking to Bethany who looked like she wanted to pry, but didn't.

"So, I had a look at your charts," she begins as she's closing the door and before I've even had a moment to sit.

"Yes, I know we're getting more tests done today concerning my heart condition and I—" I try to speak confidently, remembering that I am a nurse and a grown woman. I can handle this. Before my ass even hits the exam table, she cuts me off.

"I can tell you right now that I can make a firm diagnosis with what we have. More tests will only tell me if your condition has gotten worse in the last week, and quite frankly, I don't see how it can get much worse."

All the blood in my body seems to go to my toes. It makes them heavy and numb while my body turns cold. As I swallow, my fingers grip the edge of the exam table and the white paper crinkles under me.

"I see." It's all I can say. I suppose sometimes when you get a second opinion, the doctor can be blunt if it's the same as the first. Even as I try to embrace it and somewhere deep down I already knew, I still want to deny the truth. "So, I'll need surgery then?"

"A transplant would be best. The walls of your heart are far too thin for a repair. I'm afraid it would tear."

"Is there another doctor—"

"I am the best heart surgeon there is on the East Coast. I'm confident I can perform a transplant. I'm also confident that there is no other doctor who would agree to attempt to repair your heart knowing very well the damage to the walls of your heart." She takes a moment and I can hear her swallow before she rests the chart on her lap and adds, "I'm sorry to lay this all on you. I realize it can be a shock, but I assure you, the donor list is your best option."

"If someone dies and I happen to be a match." The reality is brutal and it picks at me, bit by bit. The chill spreads, the pain sinks in deeper. I'm really dying.

With her lips pressed in a thin line, the doctor informs me, "Organ transplants happen every day. You are not the first and you won't be the last. It's scary and not a guarantee, but we can work on other ways to keep you healthy in the meantime."

I don't want to die. It's all I can think as I sit there. It's what I've been thinking since the first doctor told me. I'm not ready to die. I just got Seth back. And now all of this?

"One thing we need to discuss..." She pauses to clear her throat then continues, "You are high on the list due to the severity of your condition, and how likely you are to accept a donor heart given the rest of your health. However, if a viable heart is selected in the next few months, you have to know there's a risk to your pregnancy."

Pregnancy? My head spins at the word.

The doctor continues speaking even though I'm stuck on one word. She's talking about term and risks and I don't understand.

"I would know. I would know if I were pregnant." I can't remember my last period but I'm on the shot. I'm not at all pregnant. She has it wrong. My head is dizzy trying to process what she's saying.

"I'm not pregnant." My statement comes out weaker than it sounded in my head.

Pursing her lips, the doctor picks the chart back up from her lap, flipping over a page, and then she looks back up at me. "Blood was taken at your most recent visit. The hormone levels were indicative of pregnancy. You are in fact pregnant, Miss Roth."

I can't breathe. "No, I'm on birth control. I'm not..." My head spins. "When did I last... My gynecologist administers them. I'm on the shot." I don't have words.

"Looking at your history, you missed your last appointment for the shot with Dr. Gaffner. You never rescheduled." Closing the chart, the doctor looks up at me with nothing but an expectant, professional look.

I imagine I look like I'm going to pass out to her. Because that's exactly how I feel.

I'm pregnant? My hand slips to my stomach, smoothing over my belly. I have a little extra weight on me, but I thought that was only because of stress. I haven't been working out in weeks and...

Oh my God, I'm pregnant. My eyes widen and all I see is a doctor who'd rather be anywhere else staring back at me.

"You didn't know."

"I didn't," I tell her with my bottom lip quivering. "I'm having a baby," I say out loud and somehow that makes it all the more real.

"There are risks," she informs me, as if breaking the little bit of a happy bubble I'm in. "I'd like to discuss your options for the pregnancy."

I never imagined I'd be a mother. How could I know how to be one when my own left me the first chance she got?

As the doctor rattles off statistics and possibilities, I ignore everything she has to say. I only have a year but that's enough time for a baby. Before I left I'd make sure that baby would know it's because I had no choice.

I cut off the doctor, unable to focus on anything she's saying. "I can't decide anything right now, I'm sorry. Would you give me some time?" I'm polite and the doctor although hesitant, complies, leaving me for a moment to simply wrap my head around the fact that I'm pregnant.

Seth is going to be a father. That's even more shocking than me being a mother.

What would he say? What will he do?

I lied. That promise I made when I walked in here is bullshit. I can't tell Seth. I can't tell Seth any of this.

It's been so long since I've been inside a church. I sure as hell won't be going today either. It's not too cold in my car as I sit here with the heat on, staring at the stained glass windows. The moment that doctor left the room, so did I.

I got the hell out of there to think. All the white sterile walls and carts... I just couldn't process it in there. Let alone have a conversation about whether or not to accept a heart when it's available and risk endangering this baby. At the thought, my hand lifts from my lap to my belly.

"You sure do know how to fuck with someone," I whisper as I watch a woman enter the church. I'm all the way on the far right side of the parking lot and it may only be six at night, but service is long over and the early evenings of autumn have made the sky turn dark.

My grandmother used to pray. She didn't do it often, but if she lost something, she'd pray to Saint Anthony, I think it was. I'm pretty sure. She said Saint Anthony helped you find what you'd lost. I don't even know if that's a Catholic thing or Baptist. I simply wasn't raised to be religious.

Yet, when times get hard, I always find myself at a church. Maybe it's because the graves are in their backyards, or that a church can always be found near a hospital. I don't know why but I drove here eight years ago when I first arrived on the East Coast and I couldn't stop thinking about Cami and Seth. The two came together, different kinds of pain. If one left, the other appeared. So I came here, to this church.

Always at night, when it's most empty.

Once, when I was little and had no idea just how hard life could be, I asked my grandma, *"If you lose your way, do you pray to Saint Anthony too?"*

She looked at me with a sad smile and crouched down in front of me. She always smelled like peppermints and at the memory, I swear I smell them again.

"When you lose your way, you pray to God."

A mix between a deep breath and a sigh fill my lungs. I have prayed so many times, and yet here I am, with a faulty heart and now a baby I don't know if I'll even be able to carry to term.

Maybe it's because I only pray at my weakest moments. I've only prayed when things were horrible and I had no way out. Maybe that's why it just gets harder. God is forcing me to keep praying.

It's a ridiculous thought and I huff a sad laugh as I sniff away the tears that prick my eyes. No more crying.

My phone buzzes again and I pick it up, thinking it's another call from the doctor's office but it's only a text from Bethany asking what my schedule is at work next week. I need time to absorb all of this, so the impatient doctor will have to wait.

It takes me a moment to search through my email and copy and paste my schedule to Bethany as my thoughts travel to all of the details I looked up about pregnant women with heart failure.

Maybe those scenarios are what led me here.

I nearly call Bethany. So many times as I've sat here for hours I've thought of calling her, telling her everything and then begging her to tell me how I can tell all of this to Seth.

How do I tell him I'm pregnant, but this baby might not make it? Oh, and I may not make it either. How do I tell him I've known for over a week now about my heart and that I lied to him?

A light in the car a few spots over goes off and then back on catching my eye. It's the security detail and I when I see the phone in his hand I wonder if he's telling Seth. The clock tells me I've been here for three hours. I don't know how. I've only been thinking. Apparently I'm slow today.

"Have you been taking all my mental energy?" I ask in a soft voice, that motherly voice every adult female seems to have around a sweet little infant. "Is that why I can't think straight anymore?" I ask this little bump.

My security detail lowers his phone and the flash of light distracts me again.

The woman is already leaving church, the same one who entered a moment ago. I wonder what she came here for and then I wonder if she has a baby.

I want a baby. That is the only conclusion I have come to repeatedly since I've been here. I would love to hold my baby.

Chapter 16

Seth

I'm a bastard. Laura can't even look me in the eyes anymore. She doesn't want to touch me. She avoids me all the time now. It's been a week of her doing this and I know it's my fault.

She's drifting away from me even though she's right here. She's always here but she's not. It's fucking killing me. All I can do is check the messages from the security detail on her. It's gotten to the point where Jase won't even have a conversation with me if my phone is out.

He can be pissed all he wants. I cannot lose her.

When I get home, her flowers are in a vase on the coffee table. It's the first sign of life I've seen from her.

For a week now. Ever since she went to the doctor. She said she's feeling sick and that's all it is, but she's lying. She goes out, she comes home, she goes to bed.

That's been her schedule. I've fucking had it. Screw Declan and his advice to give her space. It's obviously not working.

I'm not a fucking fan of *space*, apparently.

With a bottle of wine in my right hand and Chinese takeout in the other, I shut the door and listen for her.

No sign of her in the house, but I know she's here.

I call out for her as I lay everything out on the counter. I got her favorites, even the crab rangoon I think is... less than appealing. Crab and cream cheese just don't work together in my book. The wine was damn expensive and the man at the register said she'd love it. As if he knows her. Still, I got it.

"Chinese?" she says and her small voice comes from over my shoulder. She holds me from behind, hugging me first, which is new, and rests her head on my arm as she takes a look at the options. "Sesame chicken, I call that one." The smile is genuine and I'm floored. I don't understand, but she's acting normal. I'm afraid to breathe or she may go back to the sullen shell she's been wrapped up in.

"All yours, Babygirl." I stare down at her as I speak and her response is to lift up onto her tiptoes and kiss me.

It's a small peck, sweet and short although she lingers a moment longer when I lean down to go in for another. I'm granted a hum of satisfaction and then she's moving behind me to get the plates from the cabinet.

I don't miss that when she sees the wine, that bit of

happiness falls. Like it was just an act. It's already gone; the smile, the blush in her cheeks.

A worried look replaces it all and I can see the wheels spinning as she takes her time getting out two plates. One and then the other.

She's killing time until she has to go back to putting on a show for me. It's so damn clear and I can't stand it. It's eating me up inside, gnawing away at whatever makes me a semblance of a good person.

"What's wrong?"

"What?" she says as she turns around, her lips parting in shock. Both of her hands grip the counter behind her as she shakes her head. "I'm fine."

"The hell you are," I say and I don't hide the raw pain in my voice. "You think I don't see you? I know you, Laura Evelyn Roth and I know you're not happy. You're not even close to being okay."

Her sad eyes stare back at me, but the frown on her face keeps her mouth shut.

"I'm trying everything here," I tell her as I open my arms, the empty plastic bags in one hand and then I ball them up, holding on to them as if they'll ground me.

She starts to say something but then she looks past me and worries her bottom lip before catching it in her teeth.

"It's killing me, you know that? I lost you before, but this?" I throw the bags away, which makes me turn my back to her, but only for a moment. "This is hell," I tell her, the words scratching their way out of me. "It hurts to see you hurting and you pretending you're not for me."

"Would you rather I go?" The question is riddled with such loss that even her whisper mourns.

"No! No!" How can she even think that? I can't breathe. I have to loosen the fucking tie on my neck because it's choking me. "Don't leave me. Please. I want to be here for you," I say, and I am begging her. "Whatever it is that makes you cry at night; you need to tell me. I promise I won't think less of you or… shit, I don't know what you're thinking will happen if you tell me because you don't tell me anything."

Her expression crumples but still she doesn't say anything.

"I know I hurt you—"

"No, stop," she says and Laura's hand flies out in front her. Her palm faces me as if to silence me.

"I know I did." I rush out the words, hating myself. "If I could take it back, I swear to God that I would. I don't deserve you but it doesn't mean I'll ever stop wanting you. I don't want anyone else to have you and I can't walk away."

Her shoulders shake with each shuddering breath. "Stop! It's not that. Stop. Stop!"

I feel crazy and lost and reckless. Dropping down to my knees, I stare up at her. "Tell me! Please! I'm begging you," I practically yell but I don't mean to. Just like I don't mean for my eyes to turn glossy. "I can't lose you but I am. I am losing you and I hate it. You aren't here with me and I can't be without you. I will do anything, whatever it is. Please, just tell me."

Breathless and in a hell that is limbo, I watch her. She's right there, only feet away from me, but she feels so far from my grasp.

Hope stirs when she slowly drops to her knees, never taking her eyes off mine. She crawls to me and lets me hold her. That is my only salvation. It's the only way I've survived this last week; she lets me hold her.

I kiss her hair as I rock her, "Please tell me what's wrong. I love you. I love you so damn much and I can't lose you."

She has to know I love her. I know she already knew, but I can't let her walk away from me without telling her. "I love you, Laura. Please, let me love you. All I want in this world is to love you."

Chapter 17

Laura

I will never forget the way he said it. He brought it to life by speaking the words. Seth King loves me. I'll never let him take it back. He's not allowed to take those words back. Ever. They belong to me now. I knew he did, I've always known, but hearing him say it is something else. Something bigger, something I couldn't have prepared for.

"I love you more." It's all I can do to whisper the words. I cling to him, literally, holding him as close to me as I possibly can.

"Impossible," he breathes against my neck as I hold him. "I love you so much it hurts."

Till the day I die, I'll remember this moment. The moment Seth King first told me he loved me. It pains me, literally, a slamming pain in my chest, that it's because he thinks he's lost me.

"I'm just upset." My ragged excuse leaves me and he doesn't let me bury my face and hide it. He doesn't let me get away with it. I can't figure out how to tell him that if I have this baby, I will most likely die. If I take the heart, our baby will die. If I even get a chance at a heart. I choose our child. And I don't know how to look this man in the eye and lay all of that out for him. I've tried all this week to figure it out but I can't. I can't hurt him like that. All he wants me to do is promise I won't leave him and here I am, choosing to go but in my place, we'll have a child. He'll have a baby to love and I... I don't know what he's going to say. It will kill me to tell him. I know it will.

"Tell me why, tell me," he begs me, holding my arms and forcing me away enough that he can look at me.

"There's a patient and I lost her." I bite out the quickest excuse I can think.

"She died?"

"No, no. It was because of a court hearing and I'm sad she's gone," I say and wipe haphazardly at my face but my face burns with shame and embarrassment.

I can't look at him. Not in his eyes. I should be better than this. I struggle with everything now. I don't know what's right or wrong and all I know is that my happily ever after is so much different than I'd planned.

"There's nothing else? Nothing else going on?" His blue eyes beseech me and pain is there, the type of pain when you know you've lost someone.

I have to tell him. I haven't had the courage to call the doctor back. I haven't been able to fully accept it all and what will happen at the end, but I can't keep it from him any longer.

I feel like a liar. Not even speaking the falsehood *nothing else*, the lies consume me. I can't let him live like this. How could I spend this time, this short time left, allowing him to feel like I'm already gone? He'll know soon. He'll have to find out. It's not like I can hide a baby.

So will Bethany. I've almost told her so many times, but only to have someone to lean on. It's been a week and a half and instead of facing it, I've hidden. I'm not ready to tell the world and lose this little peace I have. They'll judge. No matter what I do, it'll be wrong. I just want to stay here, in this moment, for a little while. Knowing that I have a little life inside of me to love. But Seth should have that too. He should know.

"Seth, I'm pregnant and—" I want to get it all out. All at once. It's my intention, my plan. It's the only way I see it getting through to him, the gravity of it all.

He cuts me off before I can say anything else. "You're pregnant?" Shock lights in his red-rimmed eyes. His light blues shine back at me as they change to reflect nothing but happiness. I'm lost in those eyes. A gaze I have dreamed about for so, so long. It's my fault. I shouldn't be so selfish, but I don't press on when he interrupts me. I let him have that happiness. One of us should truly be happy.

His smile presses against my belly as he leans down, capturing all of me in his response. "You're pregnant," he says, no longer a question. The words resonate with gratitude. With his eyes closed, his lips pressed to my stomach, I lose it. I cry like I have never cried in my entire life.

"That's why?" he asks me even through the smile on his face. "Babygirl, I'd say don't cry, but that's why? That's why you're so emotional?" he questions although the way he says it, it sounds like he's convinced himself.

He's so happy and lost in it, that I nod my head and breathe, "Yes."

One lie. One lie. I can live with one lie to keep him here with me, holding me, happy and at peace. One of us should have it. His expression is filled with relief more than anything, but his smile never leaves. His handsome and perfect smile.

"I hope it's a boy," he tells me, wiping the corners of his eyes with the palm of his hand. "I don't know what to do with a girl, so..." he trails off and sucks in a calming breath. I don't know that I've ever seen him like this. So overwhelmed with happiness. "I'll be a good dad," he says quickly when his smile vanishes. "I swear it to you."

His pale eyes lose their shine for a moment and he asks, "Is that why you didn't tell me?"

"No, no. I just..." I would say anything to make him smile again. "It was just so early. I—"

I don't have time to finish because he cuts me off with a searing kiss. Stealing all my fear and giving me a moment with him that I thought days ago, would only be a dream. He only breaks the kiss to tell me he loves me and our baby and that we're going to be fine. Better than fine.

"We have to get so much stuff," Seth says as if he's just realizing everything that comes along with a baby.

My heart is wretched as he looks down the hall, already planning. "We can use the guest room. It's big enough for all his furniture and toys. All that... the diapers."

"His?" I joke because it makes me smile and that keeps me from crying. "It's far too early to know." Although the look on my face must be torn between the two.

"I thought I lost you," Seth breathes out. "I'm so happy right now. I don't know how I could be happier." There's only sincerity from him. No fear, no anger, no worries in the least. "Oh my God, I love you so much and now we're having a baby."

"I love you too," I tell him back and both love and hurt radiate through me.

"I promise I'll be good for you two. I swear to it," he whispers against my lips and I kiss him as hard as I can, holding him close to me before telling him I know he will.

As he lifts me into his lap, one thigh in each of his strong hands, I squeal in genuine giddiness. In this moment, I pretend. I pretend that I'm not sick. I don't do it for him; I do it for me.

Because I want this so badly. That other version of us I saw in this room the first time he brought me here, they would be doing this. Right here, exactly as we are. I want that. I want that other life where we can have our happily ever after. A real one with all the bells and whistles.

"I love you so much," I whisper in the dip of his throat and he's quick to capture my lips in a kiss before telling me, "I love you more."

Impossible.

Chapter 18

Seth

I leave Laura where she is in the bed, feeling on top of the world. She's sound asleep after hours of me worshipping her body.

Of all the scenarios I'd imagined, her being pregnant never occurred to me. Not once did I think that she was keeping that from me.

She said she wanted to be sure before telling me. She wanted the baby to be healthy and live past those first twelve weeks. She shouldn't have had to carry that burden alone.

Never. She never has to carry the weight of anything alone.

The only reason I'm leaving her now is because Declan said his news couldn't wait.

Whatever it is, whatever he found, it couldn't wait.

The entire drive to the estate, I think about how I've never even held a baby. Not a little thing.

I hope it's a boy. Although a little girl with Laura's eyes would make the world stop. Shit, my heart feels like it's exploding. I went from one extreme to the other, feeling like I was trapped in hell to being lost in heaven.

I can't stop smiling. Even when I reach the estate, I can't stop it. That's why I sit there for longer than I should, and the only reason I get out of my car is because Declan comes out and walks toward me.

"Hey, sorry it took so long," I start to tell him. Laura wants to keep it a secret, but how could I not tell everyone?

The look on Declan's face is what finally rights me, what grounds me to the paved drive of this place and the merciless world I live in. He's deathly pale and there's not a hint of humor on his face.

"It's the PO Boxes." Declan starts talking before I can say another word. He's got papers in his hands and he looks down to read one before getting frustrated. "Get in," he says as he gestures to the car and pulls the handle of the passenger side before I can even unlock it.

The car beeps softly, the headlights flashing and by the time I'm sitting in the driver seat, he's turned on the interior light above our heads.

"It's been too long, do you blame me for what happened?" He reads the first line of the paper in his hand. It's not folded but there are creases that show on the sheet.

"What is this?" I question him before he can read the next.

"Letters," he says and shakes them in his hand. "Walsh didn't lie to you. He's been talking to Marcus. Marcus is the one who knew and told him."

Blood drains from my face and I snatch the photocopies as Declan tells me, "Two weeks ago Walsh went to the PO Box." He finally sits back in his seat but he stares blankly ahead as I read the lines of letters. Some in Marcus's handwriting, others in a different style.

One starts *Old Friend*, the other *No Longer Friend*. Marcus refers to Walsh as *No Longer Friend*.

There are dozens in my hand but before I can ask, Declan tells me, "There are hundreds. He stores them there, but none postmarked from two weeks ago. He must have taken it with him to reply."

"This is how he knew about Laura and me? It's how he found out about us?"

Declan nods somberly and says, "It has to be. He photocopies the one he sends to Marcus and keeps them together. He's been doing it for years. It looks like Marcus used to give him information."

"What? Marcus is an informant?" No fucking way. My head spins with scenarios, including one where the FBI allowed him to get away with murder in order to keep tabs on other men in this world. Men like us.

"No, it's in riddles. Like he was toying with Walsh and they developed a rapport. Marcus handed over men he wanted to get caught."

It's all in riddles and ciphers and we need more time for the rest, but we've already deciphered one code. Birds are protected, dogs are men to be killed.

He grabs the papers and flicks through them before picking one and reading.

"It's heard I'll lose you soon. Are you traveling far from the woods? The dogs are barking in a way that tells me you'll leave them alone to roam. Tell me that can't be true."

He flicks to another page, the light casting down on his face and illuminating the letters.

"No, no, I've only given them the idea, I'm moving the luggage. You know sometimes you must let mutts play in order to determine the breed."

He only reads small passages of long letters. "He's not going anywhere," Declan tells me, his head still shaking as he swallows. "He's letting the men beneath him think he is in order to see what they'll do."

"How do you know?" I question although the puzzle pieces of what he read line up, one after the other.

"It doesn't make sense otherwise. You know Marcus. You know his riddles and the way he fucks with people. He must've sent Walsh a letter years ago and Walsh found a way to write back."

"We've only been through a dozen from the last month, but they talk about us, Seth. They call us birds until months ago. This one," he says and points to a page, tapping it and making it crinkle in the silent cabin, "this one has to be Carter."

He reads the first halfway down the page. I know it's Walsh's writing. It's a line that's highlighted and I can already see the page beneath it has a highlighted line as well.

"I thought you said that bird was a friend? What did the thing do to warrant such hostility?"

"The Beast of a bird went after another, taking a small female. It flies so low; it must think it is truly a dog. I cannot have it in my woods. I told you, only birds must stay." Moving to the page after, he reads, "I see the list of numbered dogs has changed, what did the one do to have vanished?"

"Numbered dogs?" I question, stopping him from continuing.

"There are numbers at the bottom of every letter, they have to be how Marcus identifies names to Walsh. We haven't figured them out yet, but between the two letters Marcus sent to Walsh, one set of numbers disappeared."

"Carter's numbers?" I surmise. He nods and then continues, switching out the page and it's another from Marcus. "The female belonged to him; you know birds have good memories. It appears they have mated." He pauses, looking up at me to say, "He took her, Carter took Aria and it put him on Marcus's list. But he took it back."

The wealth of information in those letters is dangerous.

"How many have you gone through?" I ask him and then add, "How did you get these?"

"We broke in after closing, picked the lock, and took copies. It took hours and I don't think Walsh knows, but Marcus does."

"How do you know he knows?"

"He left a letter on Carter's car at The Red Room. He was there. He addressed it, Beast." Declan swallows before telling me, "He said to tell you to bring Walsh to him." He glances at the house then back to me before closing his eyes. "It's inside. You can read it... he calls you King," he says and brings his palms to his eyes. "He said you would be the one to show Walsh to him. That it's time the two of them met."

Declan's expression is devoid of anything but concern. I'm intimately familiar with his expression. It's the look you give someone when they've been sentenced to die.

"Is that all he said?" He nods once. "Walsh wants to meet Marcus. Marcus wants us to bring Walsh to him. I need to read the note, but I am fine doing it."

"Seth," Declan warns, "I don't trust it. We have information on him, we have intel no one else has ever known. I don't think he's going to let you walk away. He could have told Walsh to meet him." He raises his voice when I shake my head. "He could do this on his own!"

"He likes to see if we'll listen. You know that. He likes to give a demand and have it met." This is the last piece of the puzzle for me. I bring Walsh to Marcus, I follow through on my word, and then I leave. I let it all go. For Laura and my baby. This is my way out.

"I have to do this," I say, cutting him off as he rambles on about not trusting Marcus.

"Marcus has been focused on you. I don't like it. I don't like a damn—"

"He has, and now he can have me."

"You could be walking to your death," he tells me evenly although his voice cracks. He swallows so harshly I know he believes every bit of what he told me.

"I could be ending this," I answer him in the same tone. "I need all this shit with them to end. When does he want to meet?"

"Tonight."

Chapter 19

Laura

"Where are you going?" I woke up to an empty bed. Just as my hand reached out to test if the sheets were still warm, I heard him in the room over.

I don't tell him I saw the guns. Seth usually leaves with one on his waistband, but he grabbed two more today. He doesn't think I pay attention but I do. His bruises and scrapes have all but healed, and I get the feeling he's on his way to get fresh ones.

"Nowhere important, Babygirl. I'll be back soon. Within hours."

"How many times have you told me that?" I question him, crossing my arms and leaning against the threshold where the hall meets the living room.

With his boots tied up, he leans back on the sofa. Blue jeans, boots, and a button-down white shirt that's rolled up to his elbows. The tats on his right arm show and it gets me all worked up.

"Come here," he says then spreads his legs and pats them. It's easy enough to go to him; it's what I want more than anything. "It's late." I murmur the protest against his chest as I breathe him in.

Whatever he smells like, I'll never grow tired of it.

"I know and I'm sorry, I have to do this tonight but then I'm staying in with you. We can be lazy together at night. Shit, we can be lazy together in the morning too." A charming smile meets me when I look up at him. "I want to be lazy with you," he tells me and I have to laugh. My shoulders jostle against his chest and I scoot in closer to him, one hand on my belly.

"I'm sorry it has to be tonight. Of all freaking nights," he says, sounding as exasperated as I feel. "Don't be mad at me." He brushes my hair back behind my ear. "I just have something to wrap up," he answers so casually, but there's this gut feeling I can't shake.

Something inside of me is screaming to tell him not to go tonight. I close my eyes and when I open them, the lick of the flames in the fireplace stares back at me. It's got to be the fear of loss. That and the guilt that I still haven't told him about my heart. The surgery isn't guaranteed. I just want to have the baby first.

The first doctor gave me a year. I can have this baby before then. Is it so wrong to keep this secret? Judging by the swell of emotion in my throat and the dreadful feeling that stirs inside the pit of my stomach, yes. Yes, it is wrong.

"Seth," I say and I almost ask him not to go tonight. I'm so close to blurting out that I need him to stay because I have to tell him something that's been killing me.

"Babygirl," he says and his voice is so calming as he repositions me on the sofa so I'm no longer on his lap. The weight of his body rests on his knee that's beside me and it makes the cushion tilt, bringing me into his body. "You don't have to be worried. One more night and after that I'm telling Jase I want to ease out of it all."

"What?" My eyes widen with shock. "I didn't ask you to do that." I know who this man is and what his life is. You can't leave the life. I'd never ask him to. "You can't just—"

"You didn't have to," he stresses and settles down next to me. "I can't leave, you're right... but I can back off. Sebastian is Carter's right-hand man. They get it and with everything going on, it's better anyway for me to lay low."

"What's going on?" I ask him breathlessly, adrenaline picking up. I don't like any of this. Nothing feels right.

"Nothing you have to worry about," he tells me as he leans his forehead against mine. "I promise."

"You make lots of promises," I whisper with my eyes

closed and my hands on his at my shoulders.

"And I'm keeping every one of them. All you have to do is promise you'll be here when I get back."

"I promise," I answer wholeheartedly. It seems hollow in my chest though. Something's wrong. I can feel it. As if I may not be here. My heart ticks and then thuds. "Seth," I say and close my eyes, ready to tell him.

"I mean it, Laura. I want to have stability. I can run the bar; I can be here more. I'll be a good dad."

There's so much hope in his voice and it's more than soothing, it's addictive. Just the idea of him holding our baby... I want to hear him say it again and again. My breath stills and I lean forward, capturing his lips with mine and surprising myself as much as him.

He smiles when he whispers, "That's my girl."

After telling me to go to bed, he says he loves me again. I love hearing it. For years I pretended he'd say it, and now I have it. I make sure the last thing he hears before he leaves is, "I love you too."

I can't bring myself to get off the sofa, but the room has a chill. So I search for a throw, but Seth doesn't have one. I decide I should hire movers tomorrow as I stare at the flowers on the coffee table that obstruct my view of the fire. The first batch I received are beautiful. The size of the bouquet is ridiculous. But damn are they beautiful. There's a mix of white and pink flowers but what really makes it are the pale blue velvet leaves. I keep wanting to touch them. They're soft and feminine and smell divine. They're the only feminine touch in this place.

I'm busy tallying a list in my head of everything to do tomorrow so I can square it away and make a new list for the baby when I drift off, my hand on my stomach.

Sleep doesn't last long though, because of my phone ringing. I leave it out in the kitchen so I can sleep easy and of course I'd fall asleep here, early in the morning to be woken up at 7:00 a.m. I hustle to the phone charging on the counter and nearly trip from my sleep-induced gracelessness.

"Hello?" I answer it after taking a deep breath. It's the hospital. No more waiting. It's time to move forward.

As she speaks, I keep my eyes closed. "Miss Roth, it's Doctor Tabor?"

"Yes, I remember," I say and my voice is even and calm. "I apologize for leaving so abruptly. I—" Before I can spit out an excuse, she stops me.

"This is not my first time, Miss Roth. I understand it can be a lot to take on. I do have to stress though, that decisions need to be made. You are very high on the list and without the transplant, I'm not sure you'd be able to successfully deliver."

"So I need a C-section?"

"Yes, we can schedule one for eighteen weeks from now, but if a heart becomes available before then—"

"Eighteen weeks? I'm sorry, but no." I'm suddenly very

awake. My hand on my belly, I start pacing and ask, "How could we deliver him so early?" I only catch that I say him after I've said it. The baby could be a her, but those semantics aren't important right now. Eighteen weeks? My baby would die. "I can't be more than a month along," I stress, swallowing harshly and waiting for an answer in the silence.

"You are far more than a month along, Miss Roth." The doctor is so sure of herself and I find myself shaking my head, my eyes closed as I brace myself against the counter.

"Due to the high levels of hormones, we estimate that you're roughly twenty weeks pregnant given the results from your initial blood taken. We could have confirmed it with an ultrasound, but since you left, we were able to confirm with the additional blood drawn at your last visit. The hormones confirm it. Roughly twenty weeks pregnant. I do need that ultrasound though, Miss Roth."

"Twenty weeks," I barely speak.

"I assure you, at thirty-eight weeks pregnant, your baby will be healthy. What I need to know is what the protocol will be if a heart is available before then, and Miss Roth, I need to give you my professional opinion. You should accept the heart."

The memories come back in a rush, starting with the missed appointment. The phone call from Bethany about her sister. "I was on my way in, but a friend needed me." That was months ago. Five months ago. I missed my birth control appointment five months ago. Next month I would have gotten the alert for the six-month shot. How could I have been so reckless?

I feel faint. I've only been with Seth for a handful of weeks. Almost a month.

"Twenty weeks?" I speak louder and again the doctor keeps talking. She doesn't understand apparently that I can't listen, I can't even think straight, let alone comprehend what she's saying. Twenty weeks is five months pregnant.

Conception happened before Seth.

Oh my God.

The baby isn't Seth's.

"I can't breathe."

Seth and Laura's story isn't over just yet.
Their story continues with
Easy To Fall.

About the Author

Thank you so much for reading my romances. I'm just a stay at home Mom and an avid reader turned Author and I couldn't be happier.

I hope you love my books as much as I do!

More by Willow Winters
www.willowwinterswrites.com/books

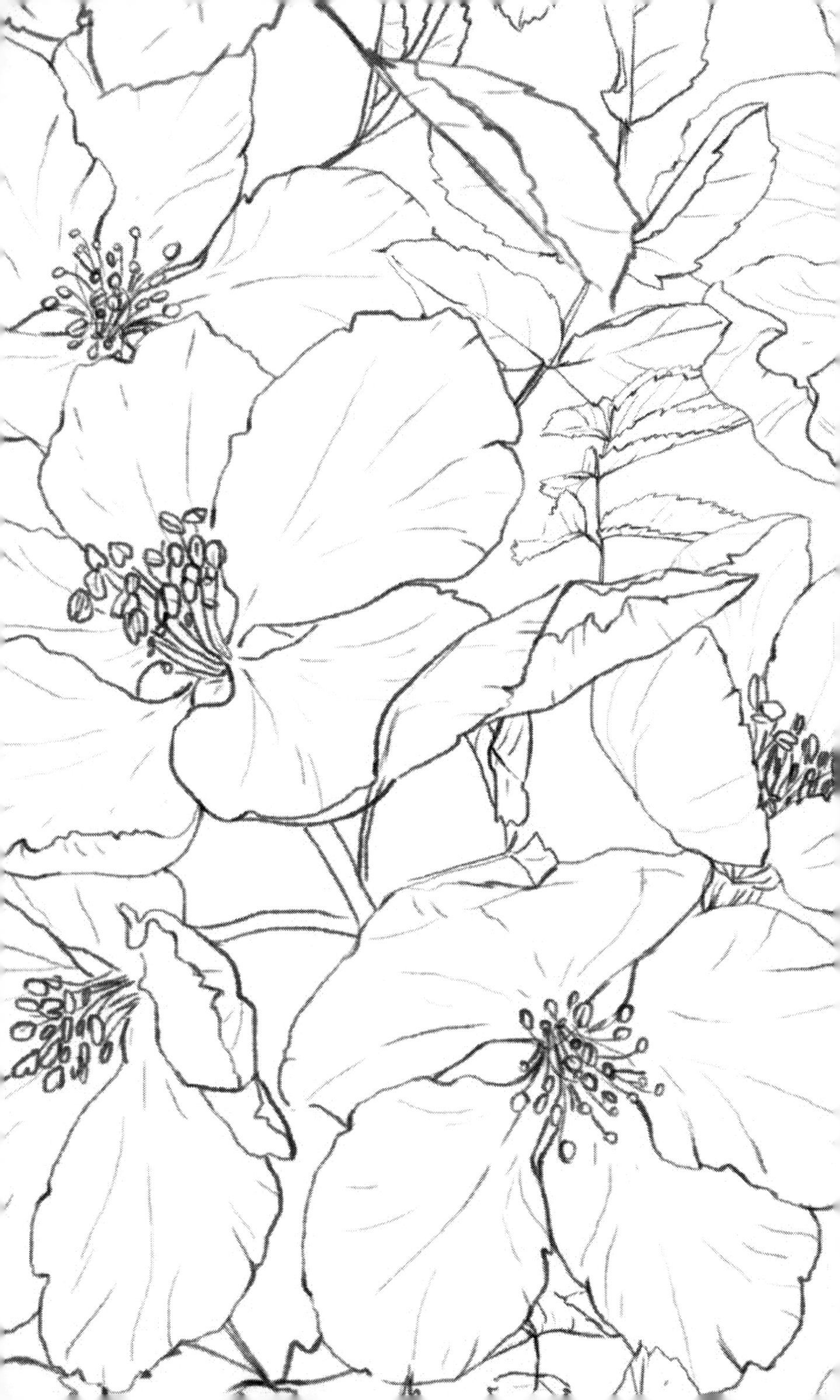

Printed in Great Britain
by Amazon